I0562965

THE PUZZLE SAFE MYSTERY

SCIENCE-FICTION COZY MYSTERY

KATHERINE OKIA

AGWANG PRESS

First Paperback edition published 2025.

ISBN: 978-1-951722-19-7 eBook

ISBN: 978-1-951722-20-3 Paperback

ISBN: 978-1-951722-21-0 Hardcover

For my darling daughter, Marta
For my supportive husband, Peter

CONTENTS

CHAPTER 1

Jill stepped from one digital painting to the next, trying to distract herself and quiet her thumping heart. Carefully analyzing Jackson's digital art, she noted how well his composition drew in the viewer's eye. The cool air of the Modern Muses gallery rustled her long, wavy brown hair as she reviewed her talking points for the upcoming conversation.

The Muses, the best of Anteros's galleries, boasted the greatest diversity of artwork, the highest quality of exhibits, and an intriguing, inviting design. It was also the largest, occupying the entire floor of the Ruby Sunset Hotel on Mars. Anteros was the only major city on Mars with a protective clear dome covering the entire city. There were several smaller galleries dotted around the city, but she didn't want to settle for them. *I have to change his mind.*

Noticing movement from the corner of her hazel eyes, she took a deep breath and smoothed her sage-green dress. Her face stiffened as she turned to meet the tall, fifty-something, balding man approaching.

"Ethan," Jill said with a tight smile. "I'm glad you could make time to meet me today."

"Anything for one of my stars," Ethan said, gathering his hands behind his back and adopting a placid expression. "I've completed the sales analysis you requested."

"Oh," Jill said, raising her eyebrows. "That was faster than I expected."

"You weren't the first to ask," Ethan said, maintaining a serene stance.

Jill's chest tightened. "What did you find?"

"Walk with me," Ethan said and ambled to a neighboring digital painting. "We have many creators who regularly feature art in our gallery. To you, it's a calling, but to us, it's a business. What do you think about this landscape of the Shadow Stone Crater?"

Jill turned and took her time carefully studying what made this image so compelling. Something about the shadowing hinted at a forgotten beauty and a hidden terror. Gazing at the indentation on Mars's surface, she just couldn't look away as the fading light played with the colors on the walls. But she wanted to shift her eyes to avoid the impending catastrophe. *Maybe it's the coming nighttime. There would be no light and therefore no colors?* She grimaced, realizing Jackson's digital image had drawn her in again.

"Jackson masterfully created this," Jill said, clearing her throat and placing a strand of wavy brown hair behind one ear. He was one of her competitors, and she struggled to match him in sales.

"Customers simply prefer his digital paintings," Ethan said. "Your paintings are beautiful, but—"

"They aren't Jackson's," Jill sighed as a heavy weight settled in her stomach.

The two of them stood in the Martian Landscape room, and she glanced at her only painting displayed there, which looked like a child's canvas next to Jackson's.

"We move ten times more of his Martian landscapes than yours," Ethan said, turning to her digital image next to Jackson's.

"When do you plan to remove my art?" Jill asked, even though she knew the answer.

"Today's the last day," Ethan said, scanning the room.

Jill did her best to keep her face neutral, hiding her panic.

"I have something else to show you. Follow me." He turned and strolled beside her as they headed out of the Martian Landscape room. They continued silently through the Lunar Terrain area and stopped in the Earth Scenes room. "What do you notice?"

"I have three digital paintings here," Jill said as her entire body tightened. "None of the others are Jackson's."

"Our patrons prefer your Earth compositions over your Martian creations," Ethan said matter-of-factly. "That doesn't mean your Mars renderings aren't good, just that Jackson's are better."

"Who else asked for a sales report?" Jill asked.

"Jackson, of course," Ethan said. "He requests regular reports. Creating art is also, at least partially, a business for him."

Jill nodded, trying to keep from screaming or maybe crying.

"Soon, you'll only have three images on display," Ethan said. "But it doesn't have to be that way. When can we expect more Earth images?"

Jill froze. She couldn't explain how much more effort it took to not just recreate a digital photo from Earth but imbue it with emotion, movement, and even personality. Each digital painting required an enormous amount of creativity, labor, sweat, and sometimes a few tears. It took several months to complete one painting, but she was nearing the end of her current creation.

"Maybe in a few more weeks," she said, taking a steadying breath. "I'll keep you updated."

Later at home, Jill leaned toward a floating screen and, layer by layer, filled in the multiple shades of blue in her current piece of art. Her hair, held in a loose ponytail, slid over her back as she leaned forward. Her dream had always been to travel to Earth and experience standing on a sandy beach while watching the waves gently roll onto the shore. But her parents weren't wealthy, and they passed away when she was nineteen. Essentially stuck in Anteros, she couldn't afford the journey to Earth with her limited resources.

She paused, thinking about her conversation with Ethan. As she sifted through her options, she considered taking more classes to learn to create digital paintings faster. Alternatively, she could try to sell her Martian landscapes in one of the smaller galleries, but they paid significantly less. She could also consider increasing her prices, but the Modern Muses might not allow that. She sighed.

A chime sounded on her comm bracelet, interrupting her thoughts. The comm allowed all citizens on Mars to access the Net, communicate with others, and send credits for purchases.

"Who is it?" Jill asked her home's AI. She furrowed her eyebrows, wondering who could be at her door so late.

"Gary Turner is at the door," the AI's crisp voice replied. "Should I let him in?"

"Did you say Gary Turner?" Jill asked, placing her stylus on top of the floating screen and slowly scanning her art space. She sat in a room designed to be a combination dining and living room. But she'd transformed the dining area into an art studio after her parents died.

She grimaced, glancing around her studio at the messy shelves stuffed with styluses, broken electronics, and hundreds of small floating images from her mom. With no time to straighten up, she shrugged and turned toward the front door of her house.

The other half of the room was the living room, which consisted of a burnt orange sofa and two pale yellow chairs that straddled a faux wooden coffee table. Jill's mom had selected this furniture because she loved vibrant colors and had passed that love on to her daughter.

"Open the door," Jill said while climbing to her feet and shielding her mind. Even though she had no abilities, some of her cousins did. This made her an Askov, and the only skill she possessed was mind-protection. About ten percent of the population exhibited special powers that allowed them to move objects with their minds or detect others' thoughts, and more. They were called Askovians, and their family members were Askovs.

She made her way to the front door, which slid open. A man with platinum blond hair and crystal blue eyes stood framed in the doorway with a perfect smile.

"Gary, what are you doing here?" Jill asked, with one hand on her hip.

"May I come in?" Gary asked in a perfectly melodious voice.

Even though Jill worked with Gary three to four days a week, seeing him in this non-work environment didn't let her forget who he really was—a Reader with the ability to discern others' thoughts. Moreover, he was an augment. His parents were wealthy enough to have him genetically modified to embody the ideal of the perfect human. But they had one thing in common: they were both orphans.

"Yes, come in and have a seat," Jill said, gesturing to one of the yellow chairs. He walked inside, gazing around the room.

"This is exactly the sort of place I thought you'd live in," he chuckled.

She bristled.

"Now, don't get me wrong," he said, holding up both hands toward her. "I just mean it's bursting with color, like I'd expect from a true artist."

She side-eyed him skeptically, wondering if she'd missed a veiled insult. Ignoring his comment, she ambled toward the burnt orange sofa while he grabbed one of the yellow chairs opposite.

"I really love your house," Gary said, looking around at the living room.

"Thank you," Jill said hesitantly. "But why are you here?"

"That's what I like about you," Gary said with a smirk. "You always get to the point. I'm here to ask a favor." He grinned broadly.

"Hmm," Jill said, tilting her head. "Couldn't you just ask me at work?"

"Well, no," Gary said and sighed. "Let me explain. Many years ago, when I was...let's say I went through a criminal phase, and I stole a very valuable piece of jewelry from my sister, Ellie. The reason I stole it was to cover a gambling debt. I always promised Ellie I'd return it, but she got married shortly after that and left Anteros. Now, she's returning after ten years, and I want to return her necklace. The problem is... I somehow stumbled into a bit of trouble again. I need you to hide it and give it to me when Ellie arrives."

Jill stared at him for several seconds, feeling something heavy forming in the pit of her stomach. *He's not telling the whole truth*, she thought.

"Look, I know this is strange," Gary said, running a hand through his perfectly styled hair. "I normally wouldn't bother you with this, but you're the only member of our team who hasn't been to the casino with me."

"You mentioned this has to do with a gambling debt?" Jill asked as her stomach twisted slightly.

"Well... yes," Gary said with a sheepish smile. "I stopped gambling after I initially lost this necklace, but I saved my wages and repurchased it after six years. But I've recently started again." He shifted uncomfortably in his chair. "This time I'm determined not to lose it. So, I want you to keep it safe for me so that I don't gamble it away."

"Am I keeping the necklace safe from you or safe for you?" Jill asked, crossing her arms. "Who's coming for it? What aren't you telling me?"

"You're keeping the necklace safe for me," Gary said in a quiet voice, keeping his eyes focused on the coffee table. "I currently owe somebody a lot of credits. I just need to make it to payday. Then I'll be able to make a substantial down payment. In the meantime, if I have that necklace on me, the person I owe could steal it. Worse yet, in a moment of weakness, I might give it to them. I can't let Ellie down."

"So..." Jill said, sitting back in her seat and examining her ceiling. "You went to the gambling casinos, got into enormous debt, and now may not be able to return Ellie's necklace. Can you tell me which casino you owe?"

"Well... no," Gary said, clearing his throat. "It wasn't exactly a casino, but was more of a private game."

"It took you six years to save enough credits to repurchase the necklace," Jill said. "What's different this time?"

"I already have most of the credits," Gary said with a triumphant grin. "The rest will be ready by the next payday."

"I can feel you're not telling me the whole truth," Jill said, leaning forward on her elbows as her stomach twisted again. "Before it was a casino; now it's a private game. My impression of those private games is that they can be very dangerous. That means somebody with a weapon could come after you. If you leave that necklace with me, they'll be looking for me."

"No, no," Gary said with a forced laugh. "Nobody's coming after me, and they definitely won't come after you." He smirked as he relaxed and leaned back in his chair. "It's not like the movies. Nobody's going to get hurt. But they're not above theft. The chances of them breaking into my house and stealing the necklace are extremely high because...they've broken in before. Many of our coworkers have been to my house and, like I said, to the casino with me. I'm sure the people I owe know all about them. So, I'm pretty sure you're safe."

"Pretty sure?" Jill asked. "But you really don't know. I could still be in danger."

"You're definitely not," Gary said, his mouth set in a grim line. "I took the precaution of using tracking armor."

"What is that?" Jill asked with a quizzical expression.

"It's just a little gadget I picked up recently," Gary said with a lopsided smile. "I didn't really think I'd need to use it, but I'm glad I have it. It rests over my ear, and it blocks the Anteros Net from tracing me when I leave my house, take public transportation, or simply walk through the neighborhoods. They have no idea anyone's even moving in those areas. I'm completely wiped clean from their system."

"Where in the world did you get that?" Jill asked, crossing her arms again. "There's no way that's legal."

"Yes..." Gary said with a shaky smile. "The person I bought it from doesn't deal in legalities. But sometimes, it's necessary not to have all of your movements monitored all the time."

"This sounds worse and worse," Jill said, her lips pinched. "There's no reason for me to put myself in danger like this."

"You're right. There's no real reason for you to extend yourself," Gary said with a half-smile as he pointed to Jill's floating screen. "Do you mind if I take a look?"

Jill hesitated, staring at the image still displayed on the large screen. After a moment of deliberation, she nodded, and they both stood while he followed her to the floating screen.

He grinned when he saw the nearly finished image and turned toward her.

"Okay, why are you laughing?" Jill asked, her mouth set in a grim line.

"I'm not laughing," Gary said with a gentle smile. "I think your work is amazing. For about five years, I've been following your work in the Modern Muses. Your lunar landscapes are alright, but it's your outdoor scenes from Earth that really capture the essence of what it feels like to be there. I should know because I spent several years on Earth at the Heliton Academy." This was a school that trained humans with special abilities—Askovians.

Jill peered at him with wide eyes. This was the second time she'd heard someone mention her

Earth landscapes. She didn't realize Gary would even be remotely interested in her artwork.

"You know that piece you sold a couple of years ago?" Gary said. "The one with the giant mountain and the sunrise over the top? A good friend of mine bought that when I showed it to him." He raised an eyebrow. "That's what I'm offering to you."

"What exactly are you offering?" Jill asked, feeling herself slowly warming to the idea of keeping the necklace.

"To expose your artwork to more of my friends," Gary said with a broad smile. "First, my friends have actually been to Earth. When they look at your digital art, it reminds them of really being there. Second, my friends have the credits to actually afford your artwork. This could be a win-win for everybody. My friends get artwork that they can brag about, and you get credits."

Jill shifted from foot to foot, seriously considering his offer. The thought of breaking out of her monotonous job and being able to work strictly as an artist while supporting herself was extremely alluring.

"Well, look, you don't have to decide now," Gary said with a sly smile. "If you don't want me to tell my friends, I can just pay a rental fee for you to hold on to the necklace." He reached into his coat and pulled out a flat, tan square box about twenty-five centimeters wide. "Please help me. I'm desperate."

Jill sighed, eyeing it and then examining her nearly finished digital art again.

"And like I said, nobody will be in danger," Gary said. "I just don't want to lose this thing before Ellie returns."

"Okay, I'll help you," Jill said, taking the flat box and overriding that deep, uneasy feeling in the pit of her stomach.

"You won't regret it." Gary laughed and reached out to hug her.

Jill stepped back, holding up a finger. "Just a minute. I have a condition. I'll hold on to your necklace and stash it in a good hiding place. But in return, I'd like you to show my paintings to twenty friends who you *know* are more likely to make a purchase."

"Done," Gary said, barely suppressing a chortle. "Where are you going to keep it? No, no, don't tell me. I think the less I know, the better."

Jill held the flat box. It was a nondescript tan color and didn't seem to have any way to open it. But she recognized that type of box. It was a puzzle safe designed to keep valuables secure. Its rough surface hid a subtle lock. Usually, the material was also indestructible or close to it. However, that feeling of trouble coming for her continued to intensify.

Several minutes later, she walked Gary to the door, where he thanked her again. She locked it and immediately walked to her parents' bedroom. She used this bedroom as a guest room, even though it was the largest, because she preferred her childhood bedroom.

Shifting her parents' old bed by a meter, she removed a piece of flooring, exposing the safe. After waving her hand over the safe's opening, it popped open. She glanced at a few pieces of precious family jewelry, her grandmother's old paintings on actual canvas, and an old map on nearly priceless parchment paper. She re-arranged some items and slipped the tan box inside.

I really hope I haven't made a terrible mistake, she thought, sighing.

CHAPTER 2

The following day, Jill sat in Izzy and Kurt's apartment, finishing the last of the salmon lunch Kurt had prepared. They were her parents' friends from years before she was born. They had helped her navigate legal steps when her parents passed away and had provided love and support when she felt overwhelmed.

"The salmon was especially good," Jill said, turning to Kurt. "How did you season it?" Animal products like fish, beef, and eggs were grown in a factory and were referred to as synthetics. They were considered cleaner and more humane than farming animals.

"Same seasoning," Kurt said with a grin. He was a tall, athletic man with a head full of gray hair. "I used a trick from my days as a chef."

"Are you going to tell us your 'trick'?" Izzy asked. She was an athletic woman with long gray hair kept in a single braid and inquisitive blue eyes.

Kurt chuckled and took a sip of coffee.

"So, I sense something's happened," Izzy said with an encouraging smile.

"Yeah..." Jill said, glancing at Izzy. *How does she always know when something's bothering me?*

"What's going on?" Kurt asked.

"A coworker visited me yesterday," Jill said, explaining how Gary had left a puzzle box for her to keep safe. "I just have a bad feeling about it. I could tell he was lying about something, but I couldn't figure out what."

"Why did you agree?" Izzy asked, not in an accusatory tone, but like someone who really wanted to understand.

"He promised to get some of his friends to purchase my paintings." Jill sighed. "I guess I really wanted to believe him."

They sat silently for a moment.

"Wait, there was something about the salmon's crispiness," Jill said, sitting up a little straighter. "Did you change the cooking instructions for the meal crafter?" A crafter was a device that assembled meals in a pantry, transformed them into energy, and teleported them to the table.

"I knew you'd get it," Kurt said with a smirk. "Izzy never understands my artistry with food." He spoke in a loud whisper while leaning toward Jill.

"You know I'm sitting right here," Izzy said, rolling her eyes with a broad smile. "You just increased the temperature for the last few minutes of cooking."

He laughed, leaning back in his chair.

"So, did anything else happen?" Izzy asked, turning away from Kurt.

"One more thing," Jill said. "I went to the Modern Muses." She explained the conversation she had with Ethan.

"Only three digital paintings?" Kurt said, shaking his head. "That's the real reason you agreed to help...what's his name, Gary?"

"I see an opportunity here," Izzy said, raising one eyebrow. "Why not create a dozen Earthscapes and dominate the art scene in Anteros?"

Jill looked down at the table and sighed.

"I think there's more to the story," Kurt said.

"Is there something we can do to help?" Izzy asked.

"Not really..." Jill sighed, peering at them. "I've never been to Earth, and yet I recreate images of beaches, forests, deserts, and more. People love my versions more than the originals. Do you know why?"

Both Kurt and Izzy shook their heads.

"I use my imagination," Jill said as a heaviness weighed on her shoulders. "You two and my parents talked so much about Earth that I fell in love with your stories. It was as if I absorbed the emotions you all felt when you were there. That's how I was able to recreate what it would feel like to stand by the shore as a storm rolls in." She exhaled as she sank against the back of her chair. "I feel like such a fraud."

Kurt and Izzy exchanged glances and chuckled.

"If that's your deepest secret, keep painting," Izzy said, reaching for Jill's hand. "We already knew you did that. It doesn't matter that you've never been to Earth because your customers prefer your versions over the originals. What was the inspiration for your current image?"

Jill stared at her, blinking.

"Kiddo, you're not a fraud," Kurt said with a twinkle in his eye. "You're an artist. If it bothers you so much, explain to your customers exactly how you create your images. They won't care."

"Or they might love your transparency," Izzy said, leaning forward. "You already have a following. Why not reach out to them and tell them everything?"

"I can't do that." Jill said, pursing her lips. "I'd lose all my patrons."

"Wait. I think Izzy's onto something," Kurt said. "We think your method of making images is fascinating. I can only imagine your attention to detail—I understand why each digital image takes months. If I received something like that, I'd treasure it."

"You really think so?" Jill asked with furrowed brows.

"Yes," Izzy said, tilting her head. "But I wish we could find a way to speed things up a little for you."

"Do you think we should alter her process?" Kurt asked. "It's really working for her."

"Well, we can address this later," Izzy said, squeezing Jill's hand. "Now answer me, what was your inspiration for your current creation?"

"A field of wheat, blowing in the wind on a bright, sunny day," Jill said with a small smile. "I really liked the wave pattern of the wheat and wondered what it would look like as water."

Kurt and Izzy chuckled.

"You think customers would like to hear that weird story?" Jill asked.

"Yes, absolutely," Izzy said, nodding encouragingly. "I think what we need is a good strategy session."

The corner of Jill's mouth turned upward as an enormous weight lifted from her shoulders.

Later that afternoon, Jill stopped by the Red Frame Gallery. She still wore her casual, short-sleeved dress with her favorite large pockets. Grinning as she stepped inside the well-lit space, she slowly turned, examining the beautifully arranged artwork.

"Jill," a short, round blonde woman said, taking quick steps. "I'm so glad you gave our little place a chance."

"Veronica," Jill chuckled softly as they exchanged a hug. "It's been what, a year? I should've kept in touch. How's the gallery?"

"Things are going well," Veronica said, gesturing at a display in the front lobby. "This is a new artist from Lunar City. What do you think of the portraits?"

"I love them," Jill said, genuinely impressed. "It's in the eyes. He...she?"

"He. Tyler," Veronica said.

"Well, Tyler really captures their emotions," Jill said. "I feel as if I can almost tell what's making them happy or sad. Very well done."

"I'm so glad you've decided to spread your wings," Veronica said with a giggle. "Follow me to my office, and you can tell me what you want." She led the way to the back of the gallery.

Jill followed with light steps, looking forward to catching up with her friend.

CHAPTER 3

Jill stepped between the rows of mechanical arms, which were carefully sifting through dirt from the latest mining excavations. It was the first day of the workweek, and she wore her red and white Spencer Industries mining uniform, displaying her job title, Quality Assurance Engineer.

A floating screen followed her as she worked her way among the mechanical arms, taking digital scans of their status and reliability. Sifting through mounds of Martian dirt, these simple-looking robots scanned for hundreds of crystal types with the help of the mining AI. These crystals included alythium, used in antigrav lifts because it is a key component for adjusting localized gravity. Eventually, she reached the end of her last inspection row.

"Hopefully done for the day," Jill said as a small smile crept across her face. Then a warning message appeared on her screen about an unknown substance.

"Knew it was too good to be true," she sighed and returned to the last set of robotic arms. Scanning the refuse tray a second time, she frowned. She pulled the opaque cover off the tray and stared through the protective clear screen, expecting to find tiny chunks of metal, probably deposited by an ancient meteorite.

"Empty. Hate these false positives." She grumbled under her breath, turned to leave the production floor, and headed back to her office.

Taking the antigrav lift from the lower mechanical floors to the upper levels, she stepped into the office seating area, strolled to the break room, and poked her head in. *Where is everybody?* she thought.

She continued down the hall and made a couple of turns, reaching her desk. Using her comm bracelet, she sent her work data from the mechanical arms to the more sophisticated engineering AI. The analysis from this AI was sent back to mines scattered across Mars's surface to make adjustments at new excavation sites.

"What's going on?" Jill asked as she gazed at her coworkers' empty desks.

"Jillian Solis," a man said. He was bronze-skinned, wore a brown IPS uniform, and spoke with a deep voice.

She turned toward the voice and noticed two people approaching. Taking in their serious expressions, her face fell as a sinking feeling formed in the pit of her stomach.

"Jill, this is Agent Harris," Angela said with a stiff expression. She was Jill's manager, a medium-height woman with blonde hair kept in a tight bun. "There's been an incident, and the IPS needs to question all of us."

"What's this about?" Jill asked, suppressing the urge to fidget with her hands.

"Would you follow me to an office?" Harris asked. "Then I'll explain everything."

Jill nodded and followed him.

Harris turned, pacing at a fast clip toward a bank of offices on the other side of the room. Traveling engineers used these rooms from time to time.

She couldn't see into the offices but realized her coworkers were likely inside being interviewed by other IPS agents.

They entered a small, windowless room. Jill took several deep breaths, fighting off a panicky feeling as she took in the blank walls. She sat at a small round table, and Harris grabbed the chair opposite. After they'd both settled into the room, Harris brought up a floating screen. He asked for her permission to record and began.

"Ms. Solis," Harris said. "How long have you worked for Spencer Industries?"

"Four years now," Jill said, wondering about this line of questioning.

"Do you know where Gary Turner is?" Harris asked with a stony expression.

Jill's chest tightened as she struggled to appear calm and relaxed.

"Gary? Why?" Jill asked, suppressing a shudder.

"Please answer the question," Harris said.

"No," Jill shook her head.

"Gary Turner's body was found at the Ruby Sunset Hotel two nights ago around three AM," Harris said.

She gasped as her eyes widened. "What? How?"

"The IPS received a report of a disturbance," Agent Harris continued. "We arrived at the

Ruby Sunset to find Gary Turner, the only oc-
cupant in the room. Someone shot him with a
blaster, and about thirty to forty-five minutes
had passed. We're still waiting for the final au-
topsy."

Jill stared for several seconds, her mind
frozen.

"Ms. Solis," Harris said. "Are you okay?"

"Y-yes. I'm just so surprised," she said.

"Do you know what Gary Turner could have
been doing at the Ruby Sunset?" the agent
asked.

"No. I have no idea," Jill said in a quiet voice,
still struggling to make sense of it all.

"How long have you known Mr. Turner?" Harris asked.

"Oh... I think he started a couple of years after
me," Jill said.

"Did you spend time with him outside of
work?" Harris asked.

"Yes," she said. "About once a week, we got
together at Leo's house and played a game."

"Did you socialize with Mr. Turner on other
occasions?" the agent asked, taking occasional
notes.

"No," Jill said. "I know he and a few others
went to the casinos sometimes."

"Why didn't you go with them?" Harris asked.

"They never asked," Jill said. "If they had, I would've turned them down. It took me a long time to sacrifice one evening a week to play a game."

"Sacrifice?" Harris asked with one raised eyebrow.

"Yes," Jill said, wondering what this had to do with Gary. "I'm an artist, and I'm working to establish myself. I use my evenings to create new pieces."

"Doesn't that affect your relationship with your team?" Harris asked, leaning with his elbows on the table.

"Uhmm..." Jill said, shrugging a shoulder. "I suppose."

"Did it bother you that, although he had less experience than you, he received more attention from your boss, Angela Newton?"

"Why are you... Never mind," Jill said, and sighed. "No, not at all."

Agent Harris's dark brown eyes bored into hers, and she felt his misdirected attempt at intimidation.

"I know that's hard to believe," Jill said as her mouth twitched. "But really, I work at Spencer Industries so I can eat. I am an artist, and if you've researched me already, you know about my displays at the Modern Muses Gallery."

"That gallery is in the same hotel where Mr. Turner died," he said in a level voice. "Where were you around three in the morning two nights ago?"

"I was in bed, sleeping," Jill said, "and before you ask, I was by myself. No one can vouch for me."

"We've already checked surveillance around your home," the agent said. "These questions are just routine."

Jill frowned, not believing a word. Like most Anteros residents, she didn't completely trust the IPS. Over the years, witnesses had made several allegations of misconduct. Nothing ever happened to any of the agents.

"Back to your art exhibits," Harris said. "There's no way you can support yourself with so little exposure. So, that makes me think you'd focus on keeping your job."

"Are you trying to say I killed Gary so that Angela would like me better?" Jill chuckled.

"You tell me," Harris said, maintaining a stoic expression.

"Well, I don't understand where you're going with these questions," Jill said, trying to gather

her thoughts. "But really, it's hard for me to be passionate about mining. I always try to do a good job. I always do what's asked of me, but I'd rather make unique digital art."

"Hmm…" Harris entered some information onto the floating screen. "When did you last see Gary Turner?"

"At the end of the week," Jill said, hoping the half-truth would distract him. "We worked together during an emergency on one of the lower floors. We had two malfunctioning mechanical arms, and it took hours to correct them. In the meantime, it slowed production by twenty percent. Any time that level of production is interrupted, we get scolded by our boss and even those higher up the chain. It was an… unpleasant day."

"Yes, I have notes on that," Harris said, scrolling through something on the floating window.

"When did you last see Gary after work?" Harris asked with narrowed brown eyes.

"The group's gaming day was about four or five days ago," Jill said, smiling inwardly as she neatly avoided answering the question. "You can check with Leo."

"We've spoken to Leo Wilson," Agent Harris said, absently scrolling through something on the screen.

"Out of curiosity," the agent asked, "when is your next exhibit?"

"Well, I'm in the middle of negotiations now," Jill said, trying to hide another half-truth. "Maybe in another month."

"We'd like you to join the others in the conference room," Harris said as he closed his floating screen, stood, and headed for the door.

Stepping into a brightly lit meeting room, she glanced at her team sitting on one side of the large rectangular conference table while three IPS agents sat across from them. Her coworkers' somber expressions and the IPS's emotionless ones prevented her from enjoying the beautiful view of Anteros.

"Now that we have you all here," Agent Harris said with pursed lips, "please tell us any additional information you didn't cover in your individual interviews. It's important that we determine what happened to Gary Turner."

"Well, Gary, he kind of liked to gamble," Leo said sheepishly. He was a tall, gangly-looking man with piercing blue eyes. He was probably Gary's closest friend as far as coworkers went, and Jill could never understand why. They seemed so different.

"Do you know how frequently he gambled?" Harris asked. "How many credits did he gamble with?"

"I only went gambling with Gary maybe once a month," Leo said, glancing at his coworkers. "Sometimes we went after a couple of months. It wasn't really that interesting to me. But the rest of us hung out with Gary two to three times a week. Sometimes we played a game, and other times we just relaxed."

Two to three times? she thought.

"What game was that?" the agent asked.

"Mystery Adventures," Minnie said with red-rimmed eyes. She was a cute, petite, slender woman with shoulder-length, straight black hair and bronze skin. "It lets you go inside a virtual world and hunt for treasure. We work as a group."

"I'm familiar with the game," Harris said. "Which environment had you selected?"

"Mars," Jill said, still wondering what they were all doing meeting so frequently. "We selected that one because we first assumed that there's no way they'd get that right. The owners of the game live on Earth." She smirked. "Turns out we were wrong."

"The game allows you to deposit items," Harris said as a statement. "Did you ever see Mr. Turner leave something inside?"

Jill's mouth tightened as she realized where he was going with this question. But she tried to hide her reaction by turning to her coworkers while shaking her head.

"We never saw anything like that," Angela said in a subdued voice, turning briefly to the others. "Was something stolen?"

"We think so," Agent Harris said. "When he left the casino, the vids showed he held a brown, flat box. It was probably a puzzle safe. But when we found him, it was gone."

Jill's heart started pounding. Harris had exactly described the puzzle box she'd put in her safe. But she couldn't figure out why Gary would have a second one.

"When was the last time all of you got together to play Mystery Adventures?" Harris asked.

"Four nights ago," Leo said. "We met at my place."

"And how did Gary seem at that time?" Harris asked.

"He was fine," Minnie said, clearing her throat. "We didn't notice anything unusual about him."

"Well, to me, he seemed a little on edge," Leo said, glancing at Minnie a few times. "He wasn't as talkative as usual. Also, he didn't eat very much."

"What about the rest of you? Did you notice anything unusual about Gary?" Harris asked.

Everyone shook their heads. Jill thought back to that day, and she felt a little guilty for not noticing his behavior. That day, she'd focused on getting the very last piece of chocolate cake. Minnie was a baker, and her desserts were always amazing.

The three IPS agents spoke softly among themselves.

"We have more to do on this floor," Harris said. "We'd like you to exit the building and go straight home. Please don't mention Mr. Turner's death until you see it on the Net."

Jill stood with her coworkers and filed out of the conference room. An IPS agent rode with them in the antigrav lift, ensuring they didn't speak with each other. Stepping out of the Spencer Industries manufacturing building, Jill peered at the clear dome that blanketed Anteros. Normally, its sight left her feeling warm and safe, but today it felt menacing, as if it hid a dangerous secret.

Even though Jill and her coworkers stepped out of the building together, they maintained their silence with each other. Heading for the public floating train, they didn't all board at the same time, as they lived in different parts of Anteros.

Jill's train was the last to arrive, and she lived the farthest away. She hadn't volunteered any information about Gary, waiting to discuss the IPS questioning with Kurt and Izzy. She hoped she had been convincing enough so they wouldn't turn their investigation toward her. *Why would someone kill for jewelry in a plain box? What was really going on here?*

CHAPTER 4

Later that day, Jill meandered through her neighborhood, lost in thought. She worried about the necklace and whether she should give it to Ellie or the IPS. Both options seemed dangerous.

After the IPS agents had sent her home, she'd contacted Izzy and Kurt, asking to meet them. Strolling from the floating train to the park, she fiddled with the collar of her old blue top. A few minutes later, she reached the empty walkway surrounding her neighborhood park. She waved when she spotted Kurt and Izzy.

"I hope I didn't keep you waiting," Jill said as she stepped into the grassy park.

"Slowpoke just arrived," Izzy said, gently nudging her husband. She wore her long gray hair in a braid down her back, while laugh lines framed her smile.

"What do you mean slowpoke?" Kurt asked, pulling a tall black-and-yellow spotted hat out of a bag and adjusting it over his short gray hair. "I forgot this, and I knew you'd absolutely love it."

Jill snickered. She felt grateful as the heavy weight on her shoulders lessened.

"It's completely hideous!" Jill smirked.

"You see?" Izzy said. "I told you."

"Oh," Kurt said, straightening his back to look down his nose at them. "Neither of you have any taste."

Izzy giggled.

"So, anything new?" Kurt asked as they began their walk.

Jill explained the interview with the IPS earlier in the day. How she had learned that Gary was dead, how he'd died, and the extra puzzle safe the IPS described. Izzy and Kurt didn't seem as surprised as she'd expected.

"I think I'm still in shock," Jill said with a sigh. "But I'm not sure what to do about it. I can't hand the puzzle safe over to Ellie. She hasn't arrived yet."

"Also, I wouldn't recommend the IPS right now," Kurt said, shaking his head. "They're still dealing with that scandal involving corrupt agents. There's bound to be more of them."

"Is that still going on?" Jill asked, glancing at Kurt. "I don't hear about it on the Net these days. I thought it was over."

"You don't hear about it for a reason," Izzy said. "The internal investigation is catching agents in higher positions."

"The way I see it, you have two terrible options," Kurt said, pursing his lips. "If you hold on to the safe, someone could break into your home. If you turn it over to the IPS, an agent could kill you to cover their tracks. I just don't understand how things got so bad."

"There's something else, too. We don't know anything about Ellie Turner," Izzy said, turning to Kurt. "We should look into her soon."

"Are you going to use your IPS contacts?" Jill asked, wondering for the hundredth time about their work for the IPS. They would never elaborate.

Kurt nodded.

The three of them walked silently for several minutes.

"On a different note," Izzy said in a lighter tone, "we attended a charity event."

"That must have been an elegant gala," Jill said, relaxing her shoulders with the change in conversation.

Izzy described the elegant gowns the Spencer women wore, the beautiful decorations, and the dancing later in the evening. Kurt detailed the food at the banquet. As a former chef, he could comment on how well everything was prepared.

"Now you must come and have lunch with us," Izzy said, grasping both of Jill's hands. "I worry about you spending so much time alone."

"I'd love to," Jill said. She didn't need any persuasion, still rattled by the IPS interview.

Fifteen minutes later, Jill sat across from Kurt and Izzy in the older couple's dining room.

"Would you like something to drink?" Kurt asked, searching through the meal crafter. "Strawberry, blueberry, or cherry mix. They're all healthy, with added nutrients, and they're creamy."

"How about strawberry," Jill said. A moment later, a creamy pink drink materialized on the table in front of her. She swallowed as the pink sweetness hit her taste buds. "Mmm... this is amazing."

"It's one of my specialties," Kurt said with a hint of pride.

Izzy sipped black coffee, and a blueberry drink materialized on the table in front of Kurt.

"Would you tell me what it was like to work for the IPS?" Jill asked after downing half her drink.

Izzy activated her comm bracelet, creating a private floating screen. Selecting something on the screen caused all the outdoor noise to disappear.

"What did you do?" Jill asked, peering at them. "Are you using dampers?" Sound dampers kept noise or conversations contained within their walls. Lower-quality dampers reduced noise levels in public spaces, but higher-grade ones completely shielded conversations.

Izzy nodded.

"Our friends at the IPS already told us about Gary's death," Kurt said. "We know there was something suspicious about it."

"Don't worry," Izzy said. "The dampers keep the IPS from snooping."

"I already knew some information about him," Jill said. "He was a Reader, gambler, and related to Angela. But when everyone gathered in the conference room, I learned he also spent a lot of time with most of our coworkers—they rarely included me. I feel as if everything I thought I knew about my workplace was wrong."

"Are you sure they excluded you?" Izzy asked in a gentle tone. "I only ask because when you get engrossed in one of your creations, you tend to disappear for days or even weeks."

"I know," Jill said with a sigh. "But I was still going to work. They didn't even mention any after-work activities."

"Maybe she's right," Kurt said with a raised eyebrow. "They deliberately excluded you. But why?"

"I don't understand," Jill said, exhaling slowly.

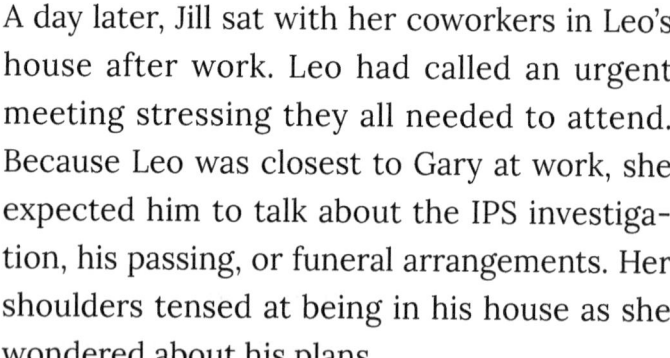

A day later, Jill sat with her coworkers in Leo's house after work. Leo had called an urgent meeting stressing they all needed to attend. Because Leo was closest to Gary at work, she expected him to talk about the IPS investigation, his passing, or funeral arrangements. Her shoulders tensed at being in his house as she wondered about his plans.

Leo was an Askov, and although he had no abilities, he came from a family of Viewers.

These Askovian family members could see long distances with their minds.

Sipping a glass of local white wine, she pondered what to do with the necklace in her family's safe. She froze for a moment when she felt someone trying to intrude on her mind. Even though Jill had no abilities, she'd used her one skill and shielded her mind before entering Leo's house. Her dad had been the victim of Readers when he was a child, and he emphasized the importance of maintaining a proper shield when in public. By this time in her life, Jill could shield her mind for days or even weeks.

She had no idea who had poked her. As she surreptitiously peeked at the others in the living room, nobody made eye contact.

"Did everybody get something to eat or drink?" Leo asked as he glanced around the room.

He lived in an Askov neighborhood in what was considered a mansion. The room they sat in contained four large sofas and numerous overstuffed chairs. The walls were adorned with wide, picturesque windows showcasing the neighboring buildings and houses. The style of the room was extremely old-fashioned, with wooden paneling, wooden floors, and a coordinating wood-carved ceiling. Although Jill was a fan of those windows, the decor felt oppressive. She took a deep breath, trying to release the heaviness.

"This is my brother, Roman," Leo said, gesturing to the man sitting next to him on the sofa.

Roman was a full-figured man with straight black hair, who looked like he could barely fit into his shirt and pants.

Jill tried to ignore the small smacking sounds Roman made as he stuffed his face with small pastry squares filled with cheese, spinach, and synthetic bacon. Leo selected the remaining hors d'oeuvres and moved them away from Roman.

"I invited you all here because there's been a development," Leo said and paused, gazing at Angela, Minnie, and Jill. "I invited Roman to join us because this affects him, too. A couple of nights ago, somebody broke into our house. I just want you to understand how serious this is. We have the best security system, probably in all of Anteros. But somebody managed to break in without tripping the alarm. The only way we even knew somebody had broken in was because some of our belongings had been moved. This includes my, Roman's, and our parents' things which were moved to various locations. I don't know why they bothered looking through our parents' possessions; they're on a multi-year trip to Lunar City."

"If they were sophisticated enough to break in and not trip the alarm, they may have moved your stuff as a warning," Angela said with furrowed brows.

"Yes," Roman said, wiping his mouth. "We thought the same thing."

"Did you contact the IPS?" Jill asked, wondering if the brothers trusted them.

"No," Leo said in a firm tone. "They're not always on your side. They can even be a hindrance if you're going against the wishes of someone more powerful. I sent a message to our parents and am waiting for their guidance."

"Do you think this was connected to Gary?" Jill asked as her face tightened. "I mean, they used a blaster on him, but this is different."

"Well, it happened the day after Gary died," Leo said with pursed lips. "I think it's reasonable to assume the two events are connected."

"But why would they start with you?" Angela asked. "You hardly ever went to the casino with Gary."

"I'm pretty sure it has to do with that missing puzzle safe," Leo said. "If Gary hid it from the smugglers, they may have assumed he hid it with one of us."

Jill held her breath, staring at Leo as if he'd read her mind.

"Well, I don't care if they do break into my house," Minnie said, crossing her arms. "I have nothing to hide. They can come and look for whatever they want."

Jill noticed Minnie's fingers trembling before she wrapped them around her torso and wondered why she was trying to appear so tough.

"Be careful what you ask for," Roman said, frowning. "We weren't home when they went through this house. But what if we had been? I mean, we know they have a weapon."

"That's a good point," Angela said, selecting an hors d'oeuvre. "They've already killed once. What's stopping them from doing it again?" She munched on a soft cheese pastry.

"That's what bothers me, too," Jill said with wrinkled eyebrows. "I almost feel like the IPS won't do anything until one of us ends up hurt or dead."

"You're jumping to conclusions," Minnie said, clearing her throat to hide a catch in her voice.

"Whoever's looking for that puzzle safe will just look through all of our stuff, and then they'll go away."

"Well, I hope you're right," Jill said, peering carefully at Minnie. "If it's like Roman said, and we're home when they catch us, it won't end well for us. Does anyone know the safe's contents?"

"I've been wondering that myself," Leo said, scratching his head. "I never saw him carrying anything extra. Also, because he's always gambling, he was frequently out of credits. So he couldn't have purchased anything valuable."

"Are you implying he stole something?" Jill asked. Why hadn't she considered that earlier? Was that story about purchasing his sister's necklace even true? Maybe he was simply passing something to her.

"I don't know," Angela said, taking another sip of wine. "Even though we were related, I've only known Gary since he was in his twenties. I know it seems like nepotism that I hired him, but he's actually a very good worker. And yes, he definitely had his problems with gambling, but never anything like breaking the law. I have trouble believing he'd steal anything."

"But he's not here," Minnie said, frowning. "Something went wrong."

"Maybe it wasn't something illegal?" Jill asked. "Maybe we're just looking at this the wrong way, like it's some kind of mix-up."

"I really hope that's true," Roman said, swallowing his wine. "At least maybe that can be fixed."

"What do you mean, 'fixed'?" Jill asked.

"I just mean that if there's a mix-up," Roman said, "maybe whoever is doing the stealing and killing can just sort it out among themselves and leave us alone."

That's not likely, she thought.

"Anyway," Leo said, "the whole reason I brought this up is that you all need to be careful. Somebody wants that tan box, and they're willing to do anything to get it."

Jill tried to suppress that panicky feeling that was tightening her chest. She mentally went through the items in her family's safe: the second tan box, the tracking armor, and the piece of paper. *What should I do?*

CHAPTER 5

The following evening at home, Jill sat on a stool next to her nearly completed digital composition of waves crashing against a cliff during a storm. She was gently adjusting the shading of some colors to add more drama to the waves when her comm bracelet chimed. She gritted her teeth but didn't respond.

"You have a delivery outside your door," her home's AI said.

Jill put down her stylus and straightened her back. *I wonder what that could be*, she thought.

"Can you scan the package?" Jill asked.

"Negative," the home's AI replied. "The package is shielded."

That familiar feeling of dread began to form in the pit of Jill's stomach. She had a bad feeling this was related to Gary.

Standing, she stretched her arms over her head and then bent over, reaching for her toes. She'd been sitting hunched over her floating screen for hours, and it felt good to move her muscles again.

As she reached the door, it slid open, and a small package, less than five centimeters, fell into the living room.

She poked her head out and looked left and right, but she saw nobody. Then she looked down at the package and narrowed her eyes, examining the handwritten name and address. Handwritten packages were extremely unusual on Anteros, and this made her consider simply putting the whole thing in the recycling. After she stared at it for a few seconds, she picked it up, noticing it was extremely light. As she stepped away from the door, it slid shut behind her, and she made her way to the sofa.

Recycled packaging covered the package, and she wondered what could be inside and how the sender had shielded the contents. Holding two ends of the package, she carefully pulled apart the glue holding the parcel closed.

A moment later, a thin piece of plastic and a folded piece of paper fluttered into her lap. Paper was extremely expensive in Anteros and wouldn't normally be used for a simple note. Running her hand on the inside of the envelope, she felt a slick surface that must've served as the barrier to prevent scanning. Curious, she turned to the paper, unfolded it, and read.

Dear Jill,

If you're reading this, I've unfortunately passed away. I just want you to know this was not the plan. Ha! Ha!

Obviously, something went wrong. Please continue with what I asked and give the necklace to my sister, Ellie. She'll arrive on the Atlas Starship in nine days.

There is one thing to caution you about. Do not, under any circumstances, give that necklace to Ellie with her husband present. Let's just say things will go very badly for her if you do. She doesn't even know I have the necklace. I was going to surprise her with it.

Let me apologize again. I'm very sorry for putting you in this terrible situation. I know you did nothing to deserve this additional stress, but I really couldn't think of another way to get the necklace to Ellie.

Yours, Gary

Jill exhaled slowly as she stared down at the physical letter. Paper like this, with no writing, would be highly valuable. She could probably resell it and eat for a month. Once it had writing on it, it was only valuable to the person who wrote it or the person receiving it. In any case, she now had another problem.

What do I do about that necklace? she thought.

Using her comm bracelet, she created a floating screen and began an encrypted search through the local Anteros Net. She found Gary and Eloise Turner, who were the only two children of the Victor Turner clan. They had been a family of Readers. But apparently, Eloise did not have any abilities.

The family appeared to be poor, which was extremely unusual for an Askovian family. Also she found that both Victor and his son, Gary, seemed to have had mini brushes with the law as they gambled frequently and got into trouble. There was no additional information about Ellie.

She wondered if Ellie even existed and, if so, whether she was actually married. Was her husband really dangerous? She blew out a sharp breath, wondering what to do. Maybe she should turn everything over to the IPS after all.

Selecting the thin piece of plastic from her lap, she climbed to her feet, still stiff from painting for so long. Rotating the clear tube between her thumb and forefinger, she ambled behind the yellow chairs, past the coffee table, and completed the circuit by going around the orange sofa.

"What am I holding in my hand?" Jill asked.

"Unknown," the home AI responded.

Jill examined the thin plastic she held between her fingers and then placed it over her ear, copying Gary.

"What did he call this thing?" Jill asked as she racked her brain. She'd half expected the AI to respond, but it remained silent.

After completing another circuit, she removed the plastic and placed it on the coffee table.

"Do you remember what Gary called that thing?" Jill asked.

"Please be advised that for twenty-point-six seconds, you were not in your home," the AI said. "You interacted with tracking armor."

"Yes, that's it," Jill said, studying the device. "He did say that he could travel anywhere in Anteros, and nobody could monitor him. I wonder why he sent it to me?"

"Unknown," the AI said. "However, tracking armor is illegal in Anteros."

"Thanks, Gary," Jill said sarcastically.

Sighing, she peered at her artwork, but she couldn't concentrate any longer. She studied the letter and the armor, feeling as if she wanted to just forget everything and turn all the evidence over to the IPS.

There were two problems with that plan. She had made a promise to Gary, but he had passed away. Did she need to honor that promise? Second, whoever killed Gary might kill her, even if she turned everything over to the IPS. There was no way to guarantee her safety.

She continued pacing around the sofa, ruminating over these thoughts and others like them.

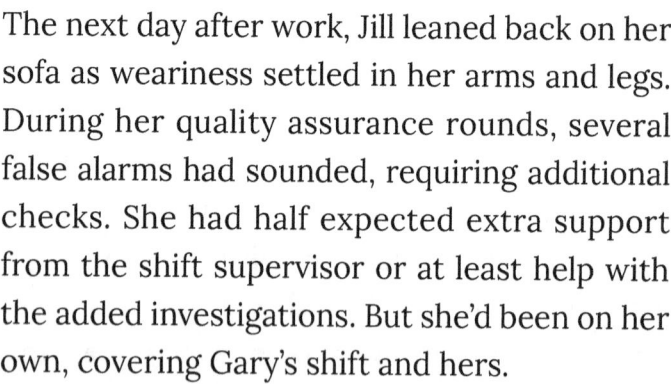

The next day after work, Jill leaned back on her sofa as weariness settled in her arms and legs. During her quality assurance rounds, several false alarms had sounded, requiring additional checks. She had half expected extra support from the shift supervisor or at least help with the added investigations. But she'd been on her own, covering Gary's shift and hers.

Looking at the floating screen next to her, she eyed a list of her patrons from the Modern Muses gallery. She planned to create a series of mini-visual memoirs detailing the making of each of her digital paintings. The memoirs would include early sketches or inspirational digital photos. On the screen, she organized her thoughts, and found the original photo, a wheat field. Next to that image, she wrote what drew her to the wind-swept field in the first place.

Her comm chimed, interrupting her thoughts. Glancing at her comm, she noticed a missed message from Minnie.

Jill sighed. Then a sinking feeling settled in the pit of her stomach as she remembered the break-in at Leo's house. Selecting Minnie's message caused a floating screen to appear over her comm bracelet.

"I'm sending this message to everyone in my work group," Minnie said, as her normally cheerful face tensed with fear. "The IPS is here investigating a break-in at my house. They said they'll be here for another hour. Can you all come over after? I just don't want to be alone."

The window went dark, and Jill closed it. A frisson of fear ran down her spine as her eyes slid toward the guest room.

A few minutes after the first message, Jill received a second, giving her the address. That message was sent to her alone, and she realized she'd been excluded from this place, too.

I wonder what they did with Gary when they got together? she thought.

An hour later, Jill walked along a broad street through a neighborhood filled with large homes surrounded by well-manicured gardens. It was the same neighborhood as Leo's, only a little closer to the clear dome protecting Anteros.

As she climbed the steps of an enormous red-stone mansion, she took in the immaculate garden with flowers and plants laid out in evenly spaced rows. The large square red-stone blocks, quarried from nearby mountains, were meant to impress visitors. But to Jill, the home lacked character and charm.

As she reached the door, it slid open, and Minnie stepped forward and hugged her.

Jill froze. Normally, Minnie either ignored or spoke condescendingly to her. Minnie grasped her hand and gently led her into the house.

"Thank you so much for coming," Minnie said with what seemed like genuine gratitude. "I was afraid no one would come, but Leo and Roman showed up just before you. I know I haven't always been nice to you, but I really appreciate you coming."

"Of course I came," Jill said with a gentle smile. "This is really serious. Someone killed Gary, and the same people have broken into two homes. I think we're all in danger and need to stick together."

"Leo, Roman." Jill nodded to them.

"I suppose the IPS has left," Jill said, taking a seat. "What did they find?"

"Basically, nothing," Minnie said with a sigh as she flopped onto the sofa next to Leo.

Jill thought they looked quite cozy and gazed about the room to stop herself from staring. It was a surprisingly modern room with large windows, large modern art pieces on the walls, and unobtrusive fresh-cut flowers strategically placed to soften the style.

"You probably don't know, but Leo and I are together," Minnie said, snuggling closer to Leo. "Our parents are close, and that's how we met."

"I'm learning so much about our team," Jill said, looking at them.

"It's against company policy for us to see each other," Minnie said, turning for a moment to Leo. "We had to hide things from Angela and even Gary. He reported everything to her."

"I see," Jill said, trying to hide her surprise at the revelation.

"Would you like something to drink?" Minnie asked. She activated the meal crafter and offered coffee and butterscotch muffins.

"Butterscotch?" Roman said, reaching for a muffin. "They smell amazing."

Jill selected one and simply inhaled. "How do you make them smell this good?"

Minnie laughed.

Taking a bite, Jill's eyes drifted shut. "Mmm..."

"This is the best you've ever done," Leo said, taking another bite and chewing.

Several minutes later, Jill finished her coffee and wiped her mouth.

"Can you tell us exactly what happened?" Jill asked.

"Yes, well," Minnie said, shifting uncomfortably on the sofa. "I got home mid-morning, and the front door was standing open. I called out, but it was quiet. I was too afraid to enter, so I contacted the IPS. They asked me to go to a friend's house, and I went to Leo and Roman's, but they weren't home."

"About thirty minutes later, they called me to return. That's when I talked to Agent Harris."

"Is he in charge of burglaries?" Jill asked, raising an eyebrow.

"No," Minnie said. "The IPS sent for him because this might be related to Gary's death. Anyway, he walked me through the entire house. Basically, I found all the family safes standing open with their contents neatly arranged in plain view. They left behind a lot of expensive jewelry. I guess the killer wanted to make a point."

"Is that what happened at your house?" Jill asked, turning to Leo.

"What? Well..." Leo started and paused. "Yes. That's exactly what they did. In my family's case, we have a lot of sensitive encrypted documents. They decrypted every device with sensitive contracts and agreements and left them open, displaying their contents."

"Is that why you didn't alert the IPS?" Jill asked, narrowing her eyes.

"No. Yes. Sort of." Leo sighed. "I contacted my parents first, and they sent their attorney over. He immediately confiscated all the document devices. My parents explained that they've instructed him to destroy everything because it might have some sort of virus. Also, the attorney has the original documents in a safe."

"I suppose the attorney's monitoring current business deals," Jill said with a quizzical expression.

"Yes, well, anything affected by the contracts," Leo said quietly.

"Basically, our parents screamed at both of us for about ten minutes," Roman said, exchanging glances with Leo. "When the attorney arrived, we explained everything to him, and he calmed our parents. I think everything's okay now, but if something goes wrong with their deal in Lunar City, we might be disowned." A lopsided smile stretched across his face.

Jill grimaced and turned to Minnie.

"You're not going to stay alone in this house, are you?" Jill asked.

"No," Minnie said, turning to Leo. "I have to wait for our security company to update all the safes. But I'll stay with Leo and Roman until our parents' return."

"If they're in Lunar City, they won't be back for at least eight months," Jill said.

Minnie nodded, glancing at Leo.

Jill wondered about the break-ins at Leo and Minnie's homes and suppressed a shiver, knowing the burglars would eventually come to her house.

CHAPTER 6

The next day, Jill was off work, and she had planned a hiking trip with Kurt and Izzy. But she wanted to finish her current digital art piece and vidchatted with them that morning. Jill tried to cancel the trip, but Izzy wouldn't hear of it. She didn't want Jill to spend the day by herself, especially after learning what happened to Minnie. After a long conversation, Jill agreed to meet them in an hour.

Jill wound her way through the neighborhood as she carried a rectangular white case. She gritted her teeth as she recalled Izzy's words, almost commanding her to their place. Reaching the Colburns' apartment, she scowled when the door slid open.

"Now, Jill, I know you're upset with me," Izzy said in a gentle voice. "But this is for your good. There's clearly somebody after every member of your team, and it's not safe for you to be alone in that house."

Jill stepped inside, paced to the sofa, placed her case on the floor, and plopped down, crossing her arms.

"I've got a surprise for you," Kurt said, beaming. "Soft chocolate chip cookies, just the way you like them." He wiggled both eyebrows.

Jill tried to glare at him, but a small smile crept across her face, anyway.

"I just need you to taste these and make sure I didn't make any mistakes," Kurt said with an obviously made-up story. He handed a stack of four cookies to her on a small plate.

"You don't have to treat me like a child," Jill said, frowning. "I'm here like you ordered." She placed a cookie in her mouth, and a moment later, it was gone.

"How was that? Too dry? Too moist?" he asked, tilting his head.

"You know they're absolutely perfect," Jill said around a mouthful of cookie. "Thank you."

"Feeling a little better?" Izzy asked, taking the chair opposite Jill and studying her cautiously.

"I suppose," Jill said with a sigh. She'd already eaten two cookies and was slowly eyeing the remaining two.

"I know this feels like we're intruding in your life," Izzy said in a more serious tone. "But both of us made a promise to your parents to keep an eye on you. And two break-ins to people connected with Gary are too many."

"Yeah, I know," Jill said, furrowing her brows. "It's a little scary for me. Even Minnie has moved in with Leo. When someone broke into Leo and Roman's house, they vidchatted with their parents, who don't trust the IPS. In Minnie's case, she contacted them. I just wonder if the result of involving the authorities will be good or bad."

"Makes me wonder what Leo's parents are hiding," Kurt said, chewing on a fresh cookie.

"I wonder if we should alert the IPS about Leo and Roman," Izzy said, turning to Kurt. "That might be an important point for them to know."

"But they're so corrupt," Kurt said. "You could cause a lot more harm."

"Agreed," Izzy said and turned to Jill. "So, should we get going? I know it's a short hike, but it'll be nice to have a change in routine."

"Where are we going?" Jill asked as she got to her feet.

"The Shadow Stone Crater," Izzy said.

A wide grin appeared on Jill's face as she thought of those Jackson art pieces at the gallery. She wondered if he'd truly captured it.

Izzy stood and strolled to the dining room table, selecting two white rectangular cases.

Jill picked up her nearly identical white case and followed Izzy out the door.

Fifteen minutes later, the three of them sat in a floating train heading for the edge of Anteros and its clear dome. It was a pleasant trip through the heart of the city as they watched the neighborhoods and parks go past their windows. In the middle of the city, a few towering business buildings obstructed the view of the surrounding hills. But that section of Anteros was relatively small, as most businesses had operations outside of Anteros, either near mines or farms. After forty-five minutes, the train reached its final destination.

The three of them left the floating train each holding their small white case. They walked just a few meters to find rental hovercars. Kurt made the selection for them, and the three of them piled into a rather luxurious one.

As Jill made her way into the vehicle, she glanced at the dashboard with a large window immediately above it, taking up one side of the interior space. These control panels were basically backups because occupants usually controlled their hovercars with their comm bracelets. The other side of the hovercar looked like a living room with a U-shaped sofa and a table at the height of a dining room table. Filled with plenty of amenities, occupants could watch entertainment serials, eat a meal, or play games.

Once their hovercar left Anteros, the three of them had lunch. They ate a small sandwich with slivers of synthetic chicken and a salad with mixed garden vegetables. Deliberately choosing a lighter lunch, they wanted to avoid discomfort from the lower gravity during their hike at the bottom of the crater.

"I've been worried about something," Kurt said, turning to Jill. "You have some valuable jewelry from your parents. I just hope it's safe."

"I think so," Jill said. "Also, it's pretty obvious whoever is breaking into our homes isn't interested in our valuables. The killer carefully arranged all of Minnie's family's jewelry in front of the open safes. Absolutely nothing was missing. That's more like a show of force or domination or something like that. Dad's safe is customized, not easy to detect, and even harder to break into. But even if the killer broke in, I hope they'd take the puzzle box and arrange the rest of the safe's contents."

"Yes, I think you're probably safe," Izzy said. "But the purpose of this trip was to stop thinking about all that awful stuff associated with Gary Turner. It's time to focus on the fun we've planned ahead."

"So, why are you so eager to go to this specific crater?" Jill asked.

"The side walls change color as the sun changes direction overhead," Izzy said. "I'm sure it's just a difference in mineral composition, but I thought it might give some inspiration for my next digital photo. I just wanted to see everything up close."

"Yeah, I've read about the amazing colors of the rocks at the bottom," Kurt said. "I'm looking forward to the hike."

A couple of hours later, their hovercraft floated to the edge of the Shadow Stone Crater. The three of them moved to the dashboard to look through the window. Jill's eyes skimmed past the tan sky and took in the crater. It was enormous, being fifty-five kilometers in diameter but only about six meters deep. The bottom was patchy with rocky and dusty areas. Jill grinned, looking forward to the new experience.

"Amazing," Jill said, wide-eyed. "I've seen tons of pictures of this place, but they don't compare to seeing it in person." The Jackson digital painting she had seen a few days ago appeared in her mind. As good as he was, he couldn't beat nature. "Is your plan for us to hike down?"

"No," Izzy said with a chuckle. "I'm too old for that kind of workout. I just wanted to stop here in case you wanted to get out and look around at the crater from the top."

"Can we just fly to the bottom?" Jill asked.

"Yes, sounds like a plan," Kurt said, munching on one of the remaining chocolate chip cookies.

"Are you still eating?" Izzy asked. "Put that away."

Kurt chortled but continued chewing his cookie.

Using her comm, Izzy changed the instructions for the hovercar, and it lifted off the edge of the crater and made its way down to the floor.

Given the time of day, with the sun just past noon, there were hardly any shadows at the bottom of the crater. It was the perfect lighting for hiking.

"Okay, let's change," Izzy said as she placed her white case on the floor and pressed the activation button. Her case gently flipped open, revealing a neatly folded, white, silky-looking spacesuit.

Jill copied Izzy, activating her white case, and then slowly selecting her spacesuit as the soft white material slipped through her hands. She pulled on the pants, which were attached to soft, smooth boots, and secured them to the belt that she tightened around her waist. Then she pulled on the top with attached gloves. However, she didn't put the gloves on just yet, but she tucked the shirt into the pants and also attached it to the belt. The last piece still in her case was a clear, soft, and silky helmet.

Izzy inspected Jill's spacesuit and then nodded her approval. She also turned to inspect her husband's, who kept slapping her hands away.

"I know how to put this on," Kurt said in a mildly irritated tone. "I don't need your help."

"Okay, okay," Izzy said with a faint chuckle.

Izzy used her comm bracelet again, creating a floating screen. She instructed the hovercar to create a room just outside the door that was sealed from Mars's environment.

"Even though we still have an atmosphere outside, we won't have gravity," Izzy said. "Be careful in the makeshift room."

Jill nodded and pulled her helmet over her head, carefully attaching it to her top.

Then she put on her gloves securing them to her top and nodded to Izzy and Kurt.

A moment later, the door to the hovercraft slid open, and Jill gasped at the new space created by the hovercraft. It looked like a clear bubble that offered an unobstructed view of the entire crater floor. A strong draft pushed against Jill's suit as the hovercraft's atmosphere rushed to fill the new chamber.

"What's the thumping noise?" Jill asked as her eyes scanned the bubble.

"The air pumps are on," Izzy said. "They're generating enough air for the bubble and the hovercraft."

All three of them stepped into the new makeshift room, closing the entrance to the hovercraft. Mars's gravity is about forty percent of Earth's at the surface. In Anteros, the builders had placed large deposits of alythium underground to maintain Earth-like gravity. Several kilometers from Anteros, the three of them could only rely on the small amounts of alythi-um in their space boots.

Stepping into the tiny room was a bit of an adjustment as their spacesuits worked to adjust the gravity on their bodies while still allowing them enough movement. They used the tiny room to just walk in circles while their bodies got used to the changes from the suit's gravity.

Once they were comfortable, they select-ed the activation button on their belts. Jill's spacesuit immediately inflated and hardened. It was a material that had been around for a few decades. Once activated, it became space-hardened, protecting the wearer from radiation and the vacuum of space. In addition, the spacesuit automatically recycled the oxy-gen and carbon dioxide.

"Can you hear me?" Izzy asked.

"Yes," Jill said. The communicator attached to the suit worked perfectly. "What about you, Kurt?"

"I can hear everybody just fine," Kurt said, turning to the door. "But we should get going."

Kurt unbuttoned the door in the bubble that led directly outside.

Jill heard the air leaking out of their tiny makeshift room, which both thrilled and scared her. Once Kurt had the door completely open, a broad grin spread across her face.

"I can't wait to get started," Jill said, laughing. "When was the last time we did this?"

"It's been a few years," Izzy replied. "I knew this was a good idea for you. Every once in a while, we all need a change of pace."

The three of them stepped out of the makeshift room and began making their way across the thick layers of dust on the crater floor. Their boots adapted to the dust's changing friction, making their walk comfortable and smooth.

"Can you imagine the size of the meteor that would've made this crater?" Jill said, excitement in her voice.

"I've often wondered about that," Kurt said. "After the meteorite struck the surface, millions of years passed, allowing the hollow to slowly fill with dust and debris."

"Ironically," Izzy said, "this is where most of the mines find crystals like alythium."

"Must have arrived with the meteorites," Jill said, almost skipping as she made her way along the surface. "I've always had a dream of coming out here and finding something really expensive. What if we found a rare crystal? We'd never need to work again."

Kurt and Izzy burst out laughing.

"You realize every single person who comes to these craters has the same dream," Izzy said.

"Oh, leave the girl alone," Kurt said, waving a hand at his wife. "It's okay to dream."

Jill giggled. She'd had this conversation with them many times.

As she made her way over the slick, dark surface, she noticed the changing colors of the crater walls. Most of the layers were variations of pinkish-tan but mixed with greens and blues. It made her wonder what type of minerals had been in the meteorite that hit the surface.

After ambling along the surface for a while, she turned back to Kurt and Izzy and noticed Izzy manipulating something on a floating screen while Kurt picked up rocks from the crater's floor and examined them with special scanning glasses.

"Are you taking new digital photos?" Jill asked Izzy.

"Yes," Izzy said. "I want to capture everything with photos first. An idea popped into my head, and I don't want to forget it."

"Of course," Jill said as she turned and continued her stroll.

A moment later, she found a beautiful blue and black rock. It seemed to actually glow. She selected it from a pile of other similar-looking rocks.

They spent a few hours exploring the crater as Jill collected more rocks. Izzy spent time working on the beginnings of a new composition. Kurt split his time between his wife and Jill.

"I think it might be time to go," Kurt said, looking at the sky's blue hues created by the setting sun.

"Beautiful," Jill said in a low voice as she took in the long shadows slowly overtaking the crater. The walls had transformed, so the faint green and blue hues now stood out as clear layers.

"I had so much fun today," Jill said. "I really didn't want to come, but I'm glad you talked me into it."

They eventually reached the hovercar. After entering, they removed their spacesuits and began their journey home. Jill chuckled softly, enjoying the respite from her troubles.

CHAPTER 7

When Jill left Kurt and Izzy's apartment, she made her way through the neighborhood, lost in thought. She pulled a crater stone out of her bag slung over one shoulder. Examining one, she eyed the beautiful shades of blue and green and wondered what she could create from the color combination. When she reached the door to her home, it slid open, and she stepped inside. Placing the white case near the front door, she held the bag of stones in one hand as she made her way to the coffee table. She'd only taken a couple of steps when she noticed something looked off.

"What's going on?" Jill asked, her voice trembling.

Her orange sofa, the yellow chairs, and the coffee table had all been moved just a few centimeters. It wasn't much, but it was enough to be noticeable. The art room chair had been scooted away from the floating screen, which was blank. It looked as if somebody had gone through the entire room looking for something.

"Was anybody here this afternoon?" Jill asked.

"Negative," the home AI said in its typical detached voice.

"Why are the chairs and table moved?" Jill asked as she peered throughout the large room.

"Unknown," the AI said.

Jill's fingers trembled as she selected a button on her comm bracelet. She wondered if she should try to back out of her home or just stand still.

"Emergency services, how may I help you?" the IPS AI said.

"Someone broke into my home," Jill said with a quavery voice. "I don't know if they're still here."

"IPS agents are on their way," the IPS AI said. "Can you ask your AI to perform a scan?"

"I'm pretty sure my home's AI has been compromised," Jill said, now shifting from foot to foot.

"Are you able to exit your home?" the IPS AI asked.

"Yes," Jill said, turning to take large strides straight out the door. She continued for several steps down the walkway while talking to the IPS operator. Turning back to the door, she noticed it hadn't slid shut.

"Whoever was in my home did something to the AI," she said, clasping her hands to still their trembling. She glanced around her neighborhood, suddenly feeling very vulnerable. A moment later, she saw a brown-suited agent racing toward her.

"Jill Solis?" Agent Harris said, a little out of breath. "Are you harmed?"

"No, no, I'm okay," Jill said as a wave of relief washed over her. "Someone tampered with my home's AI and moved the furniture out of place."

A moment later, more agents joined them.

"These are Agents Swales and Rogers," Harris said. "Swales will stay with you while Rogers and I take a look around your house."

Harris and Rogers disappeared into her home. Rogers was a tall, muscular woman with orange-red hair and freckles.

Jill waited on the path with Agent Swales. He was a pudgy man with a clean military haircut who smelled of apricot crisps. He asked a few follow-up questions, but otherwise spent his time reassuring her.

"There's nobody in your home," Agent Harris said as he approached ten or fifteen minutes later. "However, you're right—someone rearranged the furniture throughout your home. And if this is like Ms. Boothe's home, the intruders tampered with your AI." He turned back to her house. "Please follow me."

As they stepped through her door, she shuddered. Her safe space was gone, leaving a foreign and uncomfortable feeling in its place.

Agent Swales stood guard by the door while Rogers stepped around Harris and Jill, pacing farther into the room.

"In this room, it looks as if the only things moved were the chairs and table," Harris said, pointing to the items in the room. "Did I miss something?"

"Yes, my floating screen is not—" Jill began, taking a couple of steps toward it.

Agent Harris wrapped a hand around one of her arms, interrupting her.

"Please remain here," Harris said as he turned to Rogers and nodded.

Agent Rogers stepped across the room toward the floating screen. She manipulated it by moving the screen left and right, and then placed her fingers directly on the screen.

"It's been compromised," Rogers said. "It's not responding to touch or movement."

"Oh no, my artwork," Jill said, worry etching her face as she followed Rogers and stood next to her while examining the dark screen. Jill's fingers brushed over the surface, but it didn't respond. Her initial sadness faded, slowly replaced by smoldering anger.

Why would they disturb my art? she thought.

"Based on what we found in Ms. Boothe's home, your data is probably untouched," Harris said. "Considering how easily they broke in, I don't think you're completely safe here."

"You mean the killers could come back?" Jill asked, pursing her lips.

"I'm afraid so," Harris said. "Let's move to the next room." He led the way to a short hallway. Rogers followed Jill, but Swales remained in the living room.

She paused as the door to the bathroom slid open, and Harris peeked inside, then turned to her expectantly.

Jill carefully examined the position of a towel and dirty shirt lying on the floor.

"This is the way I left everything," Jill said, her face warming at the chaos of clothes that didn't make it to the laundry chute.

Agent Harris took a couple of steps to the next door, which led to Jill's bedroom. Stepping inside, he turned to Jill.

She gazed at her bed, the built-in wardrobe, and the two side tables. Whoever it was had removed all the blankets and sheets from the bed, folded them neatly on top of each other in the center of the bed, and placed the pillows on the floor.

"I don't understand this," Jill said, frowning. "Why remove all of my bedding?"

"This is consistent with what we saw at the Boothe house," Harris said, leading the way into her parents' old room, now her guest room.

Jill examined the same arrangement as her bedroom, except this room was a little larger. It had a broader bed, a massive built-in wardrobe, but the same-sized side tables. In this case, the bedding had been pulled off the bed and tossed onto the floor in a messy pile along with the pillows.

She scowled at the pile on the floor, and the anger in her stomach began to boil. Jill wondered if maybe the intruders found the safe under her parents' bed. She wanted to check but didn't want to alert the IPS.

"The only thing that's different here is the bedding," Jill said, turning to Harris.

"That's what we've noticed as well," Harris said. "Now, let's head back to the living room."

The three of them made their way there, and each took a seat. Agent Swales remained by the open door, standing guard.

"Do you consent to being recorded?" Agent Harris asked as he created a floating screen. "I'd like to take your statement."

Jill nodded.

"Do you have any idea what the intruders could've been looking for?" Agent Harris asked.

That puzzle safe Gary left with me, Jill thought. "No idea," she said, maintaining a placid face to hide her lie. "I don't even have anything worth stealing." This wasn't exactly true, as her family's safe contained some very expensive jewelry. But her dad was paranoid and had paid extra for shielding. Only a high-level military scanner could've detected the safe. Her dad's paranoia had saved the family's precious items and Gary's package.

She considered mentioning it to the IPS, but her fear of their corruption prevented her.

"Would you run through what you did today, starting from the time you woke up?" Harris asked.

Jill explained that she'd gone to meet Kurt and Izzy and that they'd taken a trip to the Shadow Stone Crater. She'd been gone for about six hours before returning.

"So that was plenty of time for the intruders to explore your home," Harris said distractedly. "Was this a planned outing?"

"Yes, planned about a month ago," Jill said, narrowing her eyes. "Do you think they're monitoring my communications?"

"It's a little suspicious that the break-ins happened when Ms. Boothe's home and yours were empty," Harris said. "I wouldn't put it past them to monitor what's being said among all of Mr. Turner's coworkers. The intruder is still looking for something."

"What should I do about my AI?" Jill asked. "I think it's been compromised."

"Yes, Ms. Boothe also couldn't use her AI," Harris said. "I know she used a company that came to reset the AI to its factory settings. That's the only way to ensure it's not operating as a conduit, relaying sensitive information. I don't mean to be disrespectful, but it can be quite pricey."

Jill nodded, crossing her arms. She refused to let the killer or intruder disrupt her life any more than they already had. She planned to hire the best company to fix the home's AI. But she didn't mention that to the IPS. Her family had always maintained a low profile by not displaying any wealth, believing that it kept them from becoming a target. Because of Gary, she'd become a target anyway, and she vowed to find whoever had broken into her home.

A moment of silence passed between them as Harris took more notes.

"As far as I know nothing's been taken from anyone's house," Jill said, thoughtfully. "Was something missing from Gary's home?"

"We're not at liberty to say," Harris said.

"Do you know anything about his family?" Jill asked. "I just wanted to send my condolences."

"There's a large extended family," Harris said vaguely.

Jill wondered why he didn't mention her boss, Angela.

He continued asking a few more follow-up questions.

"Do you have anywhere else to stay tonight?" Harris asked. "It'd be better if you didn't stay here until your AI is checked out. It could take several days."

"I'll ask Izzy and Kurt," Jill said, relaxing her arms as a new determination settled in her chest.

"Could you tell me their full names and where they live?" Harris asked.

"Kurt and Izzy Colburn," Jill said, providing the address and explaining that they were old family friends.

Jill activated her comm bracelet and started a vidchat with Izzy and Kurt.

"Hello," Izzy said, her gray hair hanging loose around her shoulders. "Jill, are you alright? What's happened?"

"Someone broke into my house," Jill said, glancing at the furniture as a look of disgust crossed her face. "The IPS is asking me not to stay here tonight."

"Well, you have to come here," Izzy said.

"We'll walk over right now and get you," Kurt said. "I don't want you to make that trek by yourself."

A tired smile settled on Jill's face as she looked forward to seeing Kurt and Izzy again.

Jill arrived very late at Izzy and Kurt's apartment, and they all agreed to talk the following morning. But Ethan vidchatted just before Jill made it to bed. She paced in her bedroom while a screen floated in front of her at eye level.

"I'm sorry for not letting you know earlier," Ethan said as light reflected off his shiny bald head. "The board met this morning and voted to move your entire Earthscapes collection to a hall behind the children's collection in the back. But we plan to move your entire collection to the featured room when you release your new image."

The trip to the crater had put her in such a good mood, and now she swayed slightly and took a seat on the edge of her bed.

"So, my digital paintings will be in a hall? Not the Earthscapes room? Why?" Jill asked, failing to keep the shakiness out of her voice.

"Look, your contract doesn't require us to keep your artwork in any particular location," Ethan said, staring at something off-screen. "In fact, your Earth digitals will expire in less than two weeks. But we'll keep them displayed be-cause we're expecting another piece."

"You haven't told me why?" Jill asked in a steady voice.

"Jackson released a new line and needs the space," Ethan said matter-of-factly. "You're not the only artist being displaced. But you're one of the few we're keeping."

Like a child's unwanted toy. Jill popped to her feet and paced silently for a couple of steps.

"Look, I really need to go now," Ethan said with a heavy sigh. "It's getting late."

"Ethan, be honest with me," Jill said, pursing her lips. "Will the Modern Muses display my artwork on the floor after my contract expires?"

"Well, it depends," Ethan said, rubbing his face with both hands. "If you release your next land-scape before the end of your contract, we'll place the new piece in the featured section. If not, then probably not. It's just business. New artists are approaching our gallery every day. If we don't make room for them, they'll go to a competing gallery. You produce too infrequent-ly for our business model. There's nothing per-sonal about this."

How could this not be personal? she thought. They were basically complaining about her method of producing art landscapes.

"Look, I really need to go," Ethan said, and the screen went dark.

"That's the last time," Jill said with a steely glint in her eyes. "I'll find a different way, if it's the last thing I do."

CHAPTER 8

The following morning, Jill, Izzy, and Kurt sat around the dining room table in their apartment, eating breakfast and drinking coffee. Kurt and Izzy had activated the dampers, preparing to discuss yesterday's break-in. Jill munched on toast drowned in butter, covered with sweet bell peppers, and sprinkled with cheese, which was her go-to comfort food.

Jill summarized the events of the previous day, explaining how the intruder had shifted the furniture but hadn't taken anything. "However, since Gary is dead, the IPS feels I could be in danger."

"And I agree with them," Izzy said, swallowing the last bite of her blueberry muffin.

"You can never be too careful," Kurt said, taking a sip of coffee. "It's obvious the intruder is the killer and they were looking for that missing puzzle safe we saw on the surveillance vids."

"We've been monitoring the case through some friends in the IPS," Izzy said.

"It's so confusing because I have an identical box in my family's safe," Jill said with furrowed brows. "I wonder if there was a mix-up. The safes look identical. Maybe I have the box intended for the killer."

"That leaves us with fewer options," Kurt said. "It's not safe to give it to the killer. The IPS is so corrupt they get witnesses killed."

"I've been worried about that," Jill said, shifting in her seat.

"This is much more dangerous than we thought," Izzy said with a heavy sigh.

"I know," Jill said, pursing her lips. "I wish I could give it to Ellie anonymously, but I don't even think that's safe."

"That reminds me," Izzy said. "Last night, we deepened our inquiry into everyone connected to Gary. There's no new information except for Ellie Turner. There's no evidence she's on the Atlas Starship, but there's plenty of evidence she lives right here in Anteros."

"Right here?" Jill asked. "Are you sure?"

"Absolutely," Izzy said, frowning. "There isn't much information on her—someone has hidden most of it. But we discovered she's not married and works for a marketing firm run by Faye."

"Really, I didn't know there was a connection between those two," Jill said with a raised eyebrow. "That might be Faye's real connection to Gary. Maybe they weren't dating at all."

"Maybe..." Kurt said, pursing his lips. "We discovered Ellie and Faye's Net information is well protected. The question is, why? We're definitely not seeing everything."

"We're still digging, though," Izzy said. "Our IPS contacts have access to a much larger database."

"What I don't understand is why Gary lied." Jill shook her head. "Why not just tell me to hand the puzzle box over to her if something went wrong?"

"Maybe it's really not safe," Izzy said, tilting her head in thought. "When you think about it, the advantage of delivering that box when the Atlas lands is that you'll be in a crowd. I don't think anybody will notice you and probably won't notice an exchange."

"I wonder if it's even jewelry," Jill said, scowling. "This is too much secrecy for a necklace."

"We were thinking the same thing," Izzy said. "Do you plan to hand over the puzzle safe when the Atlas arrives?"

"Yeah. Maybe," Jill said, shifting in her seat. "But I have another plan."

Kurt groaned.

"What is it?" Izzy asked, glancing at Kurt.

"I'm going to contact the rest of the team," Jill said and paused. "The problem is, I'm not quite sure where to meet them. I really don't want them in my house."

"Then what?" Kurt asked, as his blue eyes bored into hers.

"I'm going to start asking questions." Jill set her jaw. "I'm going after whoever broke into my house. I have a feeling someone knows something that they don't realize is important."

"But—" Kurt began and paused.

"Don't worry." Jill interrupted, her mouth set in a straight line. "I won't be stupid about it."

"I think going after a *killer* is a bad idea," Kurt said.

"Think about it," Izzy said. "Someone killed Gary Turner, an Askovian. That takes guts. Even the IPS would hesitate before crossing that line."

"Does that mean you won't help me?" Jill asked as her shoulders tightened.

"We'll help," Kurt said, putting his empty plate into the recycling. "Izzy and I will contact our IPS friends, but I don't want you involved."

"I understand you... Rather, both of you're worried about me," Jill said, lowering her shoulders with relief. "But really my plan is to tell my coworkers that someone broke into my home and ask Angela if her home was untouched."

"Kurt, that approach is normal enough not to arouse suspicion," Izzy said.

"You know how those discussions go," Kurt said with irritation in his voice. "As soon as someone goes off on a tangent, they could end up disclosing something dangerous to the intruder. If it was so easy to break into their homes, it's safe to assume they're already listening to their conversations."

"But I want to attract the killer's attention," Jill said, her eyes blazing at Izzy and Kurt. "Whoever this is made me feel unsafe in my own home. I intend to do something about it."

"You see," Kurt said in a raised voice. "I told you it was too dangerous to involve her."

"Kurt, she's already involved," Izzy said, and turned to Jill. "Explain."

"I want whoever this is to think we're trying to figure out their identity," Jill said with a grim smile. "I think this will make them complacent because they really haven't left any clues. At least, they've left no evidence that the IPS could find. Once they feel safe, they won't monitor us as closely, and I intend to use the time to work on the last part of my plan. Try to open Gary's puzzle safe."

Izzy nodded, but Kurt scowled.

"Well, the plan is less dangerous than we thought," Izzy said with a raised eyebrow. "I think we should help her."

"How do you plan to open the box?" Kurt asked, tilting his head.

"Well, years ago, dad taught me a few tricks to open puzzle safes," Jill said hesitantly. The skepticism on Kurt's face made her doubt herself.

"I remember your dad was really good at puzzle safes," Izzy said encouragingly. "But you know this is likely much more advanced than anything you've seen."

"Yeah, I know," Jill said, frowning. "But I have all of his tools. What I really need is a safe space to work."

"We'll escort you to your home and do a clean sweep for any surveillance devices," Kurt said with slumped shoulders. "I wish I could convince you to leave this alone."

"I promise I'll be careful," Jill said with a small smile.

"When will you contact your coworkers?" Izzy asked.

"As soon as we're done planning," Jill said with a grim smile.

A few minutes later, after Izzy deactivated the dampers, Jill created a floating screen above her comm bracelet and recorded the same vidchat to all of her coworkers. She let them know someone broke into her house yesterday. Also, she'd like to meet them later in the afternoon.

"Kurt and I have to pick something up to give your house a good cleaning," Izzy said. "Let's meet at your house in half an hour."

"Whatever you do, don't go inside," Kurt said in a stern voice.

"Of course," Jill said, nodding as the first part of her plan began. "I don't want to interfere with whatever you need to do to make sure nobody's monitoring me in my home."

Forty-five minutes later, Jill stood outside her house, pacing up and down the walkway. Knowing the IPS surveilled all of Anteros, she wondered what the IPS AI would make of her behavior.

"Jill, sorry we're late," Kurt said a little out of breath. "One item was harder to find. But we have everything now." He turned to her front door. "I want you to follow me inside and do exactly what I do."

Jill nodded.

Kurt stepped to the front door, and it slid open.

Jill had to restrain a gasp, as it shouldn't have opened for anyone except her. She copied Kurt's careful steps as he placed one foot inside and at the same time swiped the hair over his right ear, and turned to face her. Hesitating for a moment, she followed his foot movements and also swiped her hair from her right ear. But she didn't turn because Kurt immediately placed a clear, thin tube over her ear. He gently guided her farther into the house, as Izzy attached the same thin device.

"You have tracking armor now," Kurt said. "I didn't want you to speak until all three of us wore it."

"I thought this only worked against IPS surveillance," Jill said.

"How do you know about tracking armor?" Izzy asked.

"Oh, it's something else Gary left for me," Jill said, turning to examine the living room.

"Wait," Izzy said. "Is that everything you need to tell us?"

"Are you leaving anything out?" Kurt asked, his lips set in a straight line.

"No. I'm sorry," Jill said. "I really forgot to mention the armor."

Izzy and Kurt exchanged glances before turning to examine the living room. They each pulled a small white device from their pockets.

"I'll take my scanner to the bedrooms," Izzy said, glancing at Jill. "I'm checking for monitoring devices."

Kurt nodded and pressed a button on his small white cube. It produced a thin wedge of blue light that stretched from the ceiling to the floor. Then Kurt strolled to the center of the room, slowly turning three hundred sixty degrees.

"Clean?" Kurt stared at his scanner with wrinkled brows. "Is it broken?"

"What's the matter?" Jill asked.

"This says there're no listening gadgets, secret cams, or anything else," Kurt said. "I just can't believe it."

"But isn't that good news?" Jill asked.

"No, not really," Izzy said, turning to Kurt. "I suppose you found nothing, like me."

"That means they have something so sophisticated we can't detect it," Kurt said, pursing his lips.

"Or they're using something we haven't thought of for surveillance," Izzy said.

"Like what?" Kurt asked, studying the room. "The home's AI! That must be it."

"It's been acting strangely since this all began," Jill said as the familiar anger started to boil in her stomach.

"Maybe we should start the AI reset," Izzy said.

Kurt nodded and pulled a small black cube from his pocket. This one was even smaller than the white one. When he selected the only button on the black gadget, a thin beam of red light shot out from the cube, targeting a portion of the ceiling toward the hallway.

"What's it doing?" Jill asked, wide-eyed.

"It locates your AI's physical location, sends a reset code, but prevents it from fully recovering," Izzy said. "The idea is to see if it's been corrupted, and if it's fixable."

"Gotcha," Kurt said a moment later. He examined a floating screen hovering over the small black cube. "It has a virus." He exhaled and seemed to deflate. "I don't think we can remove it. I've never seen anything this advanced."

"If we keep the AI disabled, will it still monitor me?" Jill asked.

"I don't really know, but everything from the intruders has been extremely advanced," Kurt said. "My guess is it'll still trace your movements, communications, data, and more."

"That means we have to physically remove it," Izzy said.

"But that will alert whoever put this in," Kurt said. "There may be an advantage to keeping it in place."

"It looks as if you've gathered a lot of information about the state of the AI," Izzy said. "Let's go back to our place and do some research."

"I suppose that means I can't stay here tonight," Jill said.

"I'd prefer you stay with us," Izzy said. "If you need to get something from here now or later, always use the tracking armor."

"Did you finalize your plans to meet with your team?" Kurt asked.

"Yes, we're meeting in a couple of hours," Jill said with a sigh. "Angela says she needs to talk to us, so we're meeting there."

"I know you're disappointed, but it's best not to rush these things," Izzy said, gently squeezing Jill's arm.

Kurt allowed the AI to fully recover while the three of them exited Jill's house.

Jill began to look forward to the meeting with her coworkers. She wondered if Angela's house had remained untouched by the intruders.

CHAPTER 9

Jill stepped out of the floating train into the same neighborhood where Minnie and Leo lived. Their homes were two-story, red-stone mansions with large gardens. This time, she had to trek a little farther into the enclave, very close to the edge of the Anteros dome. This was considered the less desirable area, where most of the apartments were built.

As she approached Angela's complex, she noticed the striking views of the Martian landscape that contrasted sharply with the manicured green lawns she'd just passed. Those lawns made no sense, given the increased water required for their maintenance and the fact that Askovs were trying to emulate Earth's environment instead of Mars's. When she stepped to the front door, she paused, waiting for the AI to respond.

"Oh, I'm glad you're here," Angela said as she forced the door open. She looked so different, with dark circles under her eyes and tangled, shoulder-length blonde hair hanging loosely. She still wore her pajamas, even though it was the middle of the afternoon.

"I suppose this means your AI's not working?" Jill asked, stepping into the living room.

"It's just awful," Angela said with a pinched face. "The IPS just left. The intruders struck last night while I was at Leo's."

"Oh?" Jill said, raising one eyebrow.

What was the gang doing at Leo's? she thought.

"Come in, come in," Angela said, motioning her farther into her apartment. It was decorated in a hyper-modern style, with large windows facing the clear dome and the jagged mountains in the distance.

As they strolled into the living room, Jill paused for a moment to take in the view.

"Wow, that's magnificent," Jill said, gazing at the windows as the corners of her mouth curled. "You must see some stunning views here during sunset."

"Oh…" Angela turned distractedly to the windows. "I suppose, but I never paid much attention."

There were so many things Jill thought of to reply. As an artist, she would've made this entire room her studio and created as many breathtaking digital images as she could imagine.

"Anyway, Leo, Roman, and Minnie are on their way here," Angela said, rubbing her face. "I have to tell you, I've never been so scared in my life."

"I'm sorry to hear that," Jill said, a little taken aback by how this normally calm and authoritative woman now seemed almost like a lost child. "Did they take anything?"

"No, it's just like everyone else's," Angela said with a heavy sigh. "They pulled everything out of my safe, arranged it neatly in the open, and tampered with my apartment's AI." She turned to Jill. "Is that what happened to you?"

"Exactly," Jill said, nodding. "I think they want us to feel afraid, and it's important that we find some way to fight back."

"So far, they've targeted Leo, Minnie, you, and me," Angela said with a heavy sigh. "Actually, they broke into our homes on the same day. How did they even manage that?"

"You and I have the smallest places," Jill replied, shrugging a shoulder. "Maybe it was easier for them."

"I don't think they found what they wanted," Angela said. "I wonder what their next move will be?"

"But that's exactly what I'm talking about," Jill said. "We shouldn't sit around waiting for them to make their next move. We should do something to protect ourselves."

"Maybe..." Angela said in a weary voice as she ambled toward the dark gray sofa. She waved an arm at the opposite taupe chair, and Jill took a seat.

"You'd be well within your rights to take tomorrow off," Jill said, frowning.

"I can't. I've got too many meetings," Angela said. "What happened at your house? They also emptied your safe, too?"

"Not every home has a safe," Jill said. Even though this was true, she deliberately gave the impression that there was no safe in her house. "They removed all the bedding and, in one case, folded it neatly, and, in another, left it piled up on the floor. So weird."

"That is strange," Angela said and wrapped her arms around her torso. "I just don't understand what they're trying to prove with all of these antics."

"They want us to feel scared," Jill said, pursing her lips. "It's an additional element of intimidation to use against us."

"But to what end?" Angela asked, turning toward the window.

"They want to scare us into handing over something that Gary obviously had," Jill said, her eyes narrowing. "You, Minnie, and Leo hung out with Gary the most. Do you have any idea what this is about?"

"Of course not," Angela said, shifting uncomfortably in her seat while she gazed down at the coffee table between them.

I wonder what she's lying about, Jill thought.

"It's not as if I knew Gary that well," Angela said defensively. "We were really distant cousins who met occasionally at family reunions. All I know from my family is that Victor and eventually Gary himself gambled a lot, but I don't know more than the rest of you."

Jill paused, reflecting on Angela's words for a moment.

"You know, when you think about it," Jill said, "there's a bit of a clue about what they're looking for. In every case—well, except for mine—the safes have been opened. They're looking for something valuable and small enough to fit into a safe."

"That doesn't really narrow anything down," Angela said with a smirk. "It could be a document, jewelry, clothing, firearms, or a million other things."

"I mean, sort of," Jill said, gazing at the ceiling for a moment. "I don't think it could be anything large, like a hovercar, for example. But at the same time, it's highly valuable, which is why the safes were all vandalized. What about your safe? What types of valuable belongings do you have?"

"I'm not going to tell you what's in my safe," Angela said with a wrinkled nose. "It's none of your business."

"No, that's not what I meant," Jill said, raising a hand to stop her. "I want to know what *types* of things you have in your safe. Is it jewelry, documents, or something else?"

"It's something else, which I'm not telling you," Angela said, rolling her eyes.

"That's okay," Jill said. "It gives me an idea. Leo mentioned there were documents in his family's safes, as well as a small amount of jewelry. Minnie commented about jewelry in her home's safes. And you have something else valuable. So, they're probably looking for something non-standard, which means we can eliminate quite a few things."

"That still doesn't really narrow down the list," Angela said, now with an edge to her voice.

"Let me ask you about Gary," Jill said, furrowing her brows. "You knew he and his dad gambled. Do you have any idea how frequently they gambled or how much they lost or won?"

"Well, yeah, that was part of the family gossip," Angela said, unfolding her arms and relaxing her shoulders. "There's one story of Victor gambling so much that they literally lost their home and everything in it. Gary's mom left Anteros, and he never saw her again. The rumor was she stayed in Lunar City, divorced Victor, and remarried. There are many other stories about Gary gambling so much he became homeless for a couple of years. He owed so much that every single paycheck went straight to some shady characters."

"Do you have any idea who he gambled with?" Jill asked.

"Not exactly," Angela said. "There were rumors that it was with some casinos on the other side of Anteros. And there are lots of rumors about what those bosses do to people who owe them credits. Usually, it's some kind of torture, or they take away valuables such as land and jewelry."

"So, clearly, Gary owed somebody so many credits," Jill said, "he had to hide something from them. This something is extremely valuable and small enough to fit into a safe. How would Gary even have access to something that expensive?"

"Oh, I might have the answer to that," Angela said, her lips set in a grim line. "When Gary was younger, he was a bit of a thief. It was a nuisance when he was a teenager, and it became very serious in his early twenties. After numerous stints in jail, he finally stopped. At least, I think he did. But there are several family stories about him visiting and valuable pieces of jewelry disappearing."

"Jewelry?" Jill asked. "It's interesting that keeps recurring. Is it possible he stole something so important or expensive that the owner came after him?"

"It's definitely possible," Angela said with a sharp exhale. "It has happened before. But in that case, he was caught, the item was returned, and the IPS only detained him for a few days."

Did this have to do with the jewelry Gary supposedly stole from his sister, Ellie? she thought. *But something about that story made less and less sense.*

Just then, Jill heard someone banging on the front door. Angela jumped to her feet and made a beeline for the entrance. Jill stood and watched as she wrestled with the door before it slid open.

"Angela, how are you?" Minnie said, stepping forward to give her a warm hug.

Jill watched the exchange and wondered about the relationship between Minnie and Angela. *How could she hide her relationship with Leo and hug her like best friends?*

Leo followed Minnie and gave Angela a quick hug. All three of them turned and headed toward the living room while Roman appeared a moment later.

He stepped inside and then turned to examine the door.

"Will this close on its own, or should I try to do something?" Roman asked.

"No, it closes eventually," Angela said. "But it just won't open automatically."

Roman trailed the others into the room and grabbed a soft white chair opposite the sofa.

Leo, Angela, and Minnie sat together on the sofa as they quietly commiserated about their homes being broken into.

"Jill, what do you think of all this?" Minnie asked with piercing brown eyes.

"Angela and I have just been talking about it," Jill said, tilting her head thoughtfully. "So far, my best guess is Gary got in trouble with somebody who is at least as dangerous as the casino bosses. There's a high probability that he stole something valuable, like jewelry. They clearly want it back, which is why they're breaking into our homes."

"This all seems very unlikely," Leo said, scoffing. "I'm probably the person who spent the most time with the man. Except for gambling, he was kind of lazy. I can't see him going out of his way to steal anything."

"Well, I'm definitely open to any other theories," Jill said with a lopsided smile. "I didn't know him as well as the rest of you."

"Here's my theory," Roman said, his eyes narrowing. "From the little I knew about Gary, I would describe him as opportunistic. It's true, he wouldn't go out of his way to commit a robbery. But if he's accidentally in the right place at the right time, he's going to take the shortcut. If it means he can pocket something, tell a white lie, or just withhold valuable information, he'll do it. I think he did something like that, but to the wrong person who absolutely couldn't forgive."

"I like your theory," Jill said, warming to Roman's idea. "But where did he run into the wrong person?"

"My guess would be someone he met while gambling," Roman said. "There are all sorts of people who go to those casinos, and not all of them are above breaking the law."

"I think the two of you have been watching too many entertainment serials," Leo said with a small chuckle. "That's the sort of stuff that happens on *The Twilight* or *The Dark Embers*."

"Well, I have a theory, too," Minnie said in a soft voice. "Gary had several girlfriends."

Jill raised her eyebrows, Leo stiffened, and Angela looked away. Only Roman seemed completely unsurprised.

"I was out at that nice restaurant across from the Blue Sun Casino," Minnie said and turned to Leo. "What's it called?"

Leo shrugged a shoulder.

"Anyway, it was Betty's birthday, and a small group of us were there," Minnie said, warming to her story. "Gary walked in with this stunning, tall woman. He didn't notice us and seemed to focus only on her."

A moment of silence passed as Leo and Roman exchanged glances.

"I noticed that look between you two," Angela said, her eyes boring into Leo and Roman. "You know something?"

Jill looked between the two men, but she didn't need them to say anything. They already knew who else Gary was seeing.

"Do either one of you want to offer up any names?" Angela asked. "Let me remind you, someone has broken into our homes. We're all in danger!"

Leo shifted uncomfortably in his seat. Roman opened his mouth as if he was going to say something. But Jill caught Leo's head shake, and Roman closed his mouth.

"There's a real chance that whoever Gary was seeing could have had access to a really dangerous person," Jill said, addressing Leo and Roman.

The three women stared at Leo.

"Okay, all I've got is a name," Leo said defensively. "It's Faye. She's a tall, black-haired, augmented woman, and that's all I've got. I don't know where he met her, where they went, nothing. He never told us."

"I know her last name is Overton," Roman said in a quiet voice. "I tried to follow her once, and I caught the identification of a huge hovercar that picked her up. But her information is locked down pretty well on the Net, so she's very difficult to research."

"Well, a name is a start," Jill said with one raised eyebrow. "Maybe we can start our research there."

"Wait," Leo said, holding up both hands. "What are you talking about? We can't go researching this. Gary is dead!"

"Exactly," Jill said, her eyes boring into Leo's. "These people have killed a friend, and the IPS isn't doing much about it. Nobody's coming to help us; we have to do this ourselves. I suggest the five of us pool our resources and start digging."

CHAPTER 10

Two days later, Jill made her way across one of the underground mechanical floors of the Spencer Industries manufacturing buildings. It was her first day back at work after being off for three days. She felt as if her feet were dragging along the floor. Worse yet, Angela had assigned her regular rotation as well as Gary's again. She struggled to maintain her enthusiasm for her job, which often seemed like mindless drudgery. But it allowed her to maintain her lifestyle, so she really couldn't complain.

Her job was really to check on the quality assurance AI. This AI analyzed the waste rock remaining from the mechanical robots' previous sorts. The goal of every round of sifting through mined rubble was to find any stray crystals. In all her years working for Spencer Industries, she'd never found anything larger than a crystal shard.

The only thing that caused regular disruptions was that the quality control AI wasn't programmed to handle unknown substances. A good day for Jill, as she made it through her inspections, was finding zero unknown substances. But that only happened once or twice per week.

"Halfway there," Jill muttered under her breath as she tried to encourage herself to keep going. Her rotation plus Gary's was taking twice as long as usual.

Jill glanced at the floating screen that followed her as she completed her rounds and started on Gary's. As she paced through the first level of his rounds, she spotted an unknown substance warning. She sighed, wishing she could go back home and resume working on her digital art. Seriously considering ignoring the warning, she stood still among the working robotic arms. Every once in a while, the substance would be worth a lot of credits, but usually, it was debris from an ancient meteorite that only scientists would be interested in. Also, Spencer Industries would fire her if they knew she'd deliberately left something valuable in the refuse tray.

After weighing her options about earning credits to support herself, she pursed her lips, spun on her heel, and marched back to the refuse tray below the last mechanical arm she'd inspected. She yanked open the covered tray, expecting to find tiny flecks of stone. Instead, she found four neatly arranged, shiny, clear crystals. Jill gasped.

"What in the world?" she whispered. The first unusual thing about these crystals was their size, about two to three centimeters each. The second unusual thing was the location. This was Gary's regular rotation. Staring at them for a moment, she wondered what she should do.

There's no way the sorters missed crystals this large, she thought. *Someone placed or teleported them here.* Teleportation in this case would work the same way a meal crafter sends food from the pantry to the table.

Glancing at the cams surveilling the floor, Jill removed a hand scanner from her belt and set it to private so that the results wouldn't be recorded. Then she ran the scanner over the crystals.

"Galzium?" she said in a low voice and shivered. These crystals weren't an unknown substance, and someone was coming for them. Galzium was an extremely rare mineral found in specific mineral pockets on Mars. Recently, scientists discovered that it was an extremely efficient energy source, but because there was such a small quantity of it, mostly the military and key scientists had access to it. When a large corporation like Spencer Industries came across the crystal, they were supposed to turn it over to the military. But there were many rumors that these crystals were really sold on the black market.

Now she wondered what she should do about them. Protocol required her to place them in a radiation-hardened container and deposit them in a collection slot on the other side of the floor. But if Gary was part of a smuggling ring, the galzium would alert them that she knew about the high-value crystals, which would put her in danger. If she left them where they were, the group could see her unknown substance alerts and figure out she knew about the galzium. A frisson of fear raced down her spine. She decided to take them and turn them over to the

IPS. That way, there'd be a public record of her, the IPS, and the rare crystals.

Jill inserted trembling hands through the protective gloves on the side of the refuse container. Gazing through the clear top, she selected a flat, black, radiation-hardened bag, swept the four crystals inside, and sealed it.

The refuse container initiated a procedure to remove any residual radiation contamination. When the container door opened with a hiss, she carefully removed two bags, one hidden under the other, making sure they appeared to be one. Her knees wobbled as she strolled toward the collection slot. She held both bags together so it wouldn't be obvious there were two. Halfway there, she stumbled and fell to her knees. As quickly as possible, she stuffed one of the bags up her sleeve, climbed to her feet, and continued walking. She shoved the remaining bag into the wall slot and turned to the lifts.

Sending a message to Angela, she made her way to the antigrav lifts. Her message alerted her boss that she wasn't feeling well. She felt a little confident that if Angela reviewed the cams, she'd see Jill's fall, supporting her illness claim.

A moment later, she rode the lift to the first floor, and stepped out of the building, doing her best to walk as casually as possible. Next, she headed straight for the floating train. Taking the train back to her neighborhood, she breathed a sigh of relief, but she couldn't completely relax until she was at the Colburns' apartment. Exiting the train, she made her way to Kurt and Izzy's apartment. As she approached the front door, it slid open, and she walked in.

"Izzy, Kurt," Jill called out, hoping they were home.

Izzy sat on a stool, bent over a floating screen. Jill immediately recognized the photos from their hike to Shadow Stone Crater.

"Oh, they're beautiful," Jill said with a small smile. "You must have captured a lot; I haven't seen all of them."

"What are you doing back so soon?" Kurt asked, sitting up from the sofa where he'd been reclining with an entertainment serial.

"Something wrong?" Izzy asked with a raised eyebrow.

"I'm in a little trouble," Jill said, the corners of her mouth turning down.

Kurt patted the seat next to him while Izzy made her way to an opposite chair.

Jill explained that today, she had walked her rounds as well as Gary's. Describing what she'd found, she realized probably more than one person was smuggling these crystals out of the mine. She was afraid that if she left them there, the smugglers would realize she had found them. If she deposited them with a shift supervisor, they'd know she knew. So, she decided to turn them over to the IPS.

"Yes, that's a good idea," Izzy said. "It puts the focus back on the criminal ring and keeps you away from danger."

"Now hold on," Kurt said, setting his lips in a grim line. "Whoever we contact from the IPS could decide to take the crystals and kill all three of us. They may even claim you stole them because you didn't turn them in to a supervisor like you were supposed to."

"I considered that," Jill said. "But Agent Harris seemed trustworthy. Even your contacts said the same thing."

"We could ask them to send more than one agent," Izzy said thoughtfully.

"What would we tell them?" Jill asked.

"Hmm..." Kurt said. "We could ask our friends in the IPS to make sure multiple agents show up."

"But they're still going to need a good reason," Izzy said. "I say we tell them the truth, but not the whole truth, of course."

"I thought we should meet in a public area," Jill said. "Someplace like the park would be good because of the continuous surveillance."

"Okay, when should we do this?" Kurt asked.

"Now," Jill said, chewing on her bottom lip. "I don't think I'll be safe until I can hand this over as publicly as possible."

Kurt contacted a friend in the IPS and asked him to get Harris to the neighborhood park. They had important information for him.

The three of them left the apartment and took the short walk to the park. On their way, they continued their conversation.

"Galzium is very rare," Kurt said. "Usually, you find it in micro-sizes. Four solid crystals means somebody found a vein. More importantly, they didn't alert the authorities."

"I think it's clear Gary was part of a smuggling ring," Izzy said, turning to Jill. "Normally, do you have to deposit your findings with Angela?"

"No, not her," Jill said. "There are several shift supervisors who report to her. They rotate weekly, and I'm not sure who was supposed to be there last week."

When the three of them reached the park, they started their weekly walking circuit around the small pond, past a copse of trees, near the playground, and ending in the open grassy field where they started.

"Mr. and Ms. Colburn, Ms. Solis," Agent Harris said as a greeting, approaching them. "I came as soon as I could."

"Let's have a seat," Kurt said, directing everyone to a nearby set of tables with benches on both sides.

They sat on one side, while the agent sat across the table. Jill quickly spotted two cams pointing roughly in their direction.

"Would you mind if I recorded our conversation?" Harris asked.

All three immediately agreed, and Jill began describing her workday and what she'd discovered in the refuse tray. She also explained that she felt she was in danger, which was why she wanted to turn the crystals over to the IPS.

Harris stared at the three of them for several seconds before turning to his floating screen to add more notes. "I've alerted headquarters that I need backup." He cleared his throat. "I know this may not give you much confidence, but the last time we uncovered a smuggling ring, several agents died. I'm following protocol and alerting as many agents as possible."

Jill exchanged glances with Izzy. She wouldn't expect an agent to be in danger, too. Several rumors about IPS corruption crossed her mind.

The four of them remained on the bench while children played on the distant playground. A group of Movers played a ball game that involved using their minds to get a ball through a randomly moving hoop.

Several minutes later, seven uniformed IPS agents approached. Jill recognized Swales' heavyset frame and Rogers' freckled face. They followed a woman with wrinkles around her eyes and her hair in a loose bun. Harris stood to greet the group and summarized Jill's words. After a moment, they approached.

"Ms. Solis, this is my supervisor, Agent Leigh," Harris said. They all exchanged greetings. Harris regained his seat.

"Do you have the crystals?" Leigh asked, taking a seat next to Harris.

Jill reached into her jacket pocket and removed a thin, black bag. "Don't worry, it's radiation-hardened."

"Ms. Solis, I understand why you turned these crystals over to us," Leigh said. "We need to report this to several entities, including Spencer Industries. They may retaliate with a lawsuit."

"I know," Jill said, scowling. "I just don't trust Spencer."

Leigh asked a few more follow-up questions before the IPS agents left.

"I've been wondering something," Jill said. "Why was Gary killed? Surely, it would've been better to wait until he completed his last delivery."

CHAPTER 11

Early the next morning, Jill sipped coffee in Izzy and Kurt's guest bedroom. Composing a message to her patrons at the Modern Muses Gallery, she suppressed a sigh. She wished she'd been more diligent at gathering her customers' information. Now, she was determined to stay in contact with the few who were loyal enough to purchase from her. A knock on the door interrupted her thoughts.

"Yes," Jill said, turning to the door that slid open.

"You're up early," Izzy said, covering her mouth to hide her yawn.

"Yeah, just sending a quick message," Jill said with a note of determination. "I've decided to stay in regular contact with the people who actually buy from me. I've started a visual memoir for each of my works. Only those on my list will be eligible for early copies."

"Oh, I'm glad you've started that," Izzy said, tilting her head. "How will you get others to join your list?"

"I'm already talking with Veronica at the Red Frame Gallery," Jill said. "We're hashing out the details for a showing."

"Good," Izzy said with an encouraging smile, "I like that you're not sitting around waiting for Ethan to throw you some crumbs."

"Exactly!" Jill said with a nod.

"Kurt and I were thinking of breakfast," Izzy said. "Are you hungry?"

"Not right now," Jill said. "I want to work on a compelling message."

"Very well," Izzy said, turning to leave. "We'll see you soon."

Jill nodded and began working on a message to her patrons, offering a visual memoir.

An hour later, Jill joined Kurt and Izzy for breakfast in their dining room. They read a notice on a floating screen on a wall near the table that had interrupted their entertainment serial.

Breaking News: Spencer Industries has come under scrutiny for hiding a newly discovered

vein of galzium. Their failure to disclose the dis-
covery has brought them into direct conflict with
the Martian and Earth military forces. News
sources reached out to the local Spencer Indus-
tries president. He responded that he couldn't
reply due to the evolving nature of the investiga-
tion.

"Well, that didn't take long," Jill said, holding her cup of coffee halfway to her mouth. "The IPS must have gone straight to Spencer Industries with the evidence."

"Well," Kurt said, shaking his head. "Harris mentioned that the last time the IPS sat on evidence, valuable agents died."

"I noticed this time they even approached news agencies," Izzy said. "It was a good move because last time Spencer—or was that Pendleton Mining—tried to sweep it all under the rug." The two largest mining corporations were Spencer Industries and Pendleton Mining. Each company was created by the Spencer and Pendleton Askovian families, respectively.

"I suppose someone at work is a killer," Jill said, swallowing the last of her coffee. "But why Gary? If I found those crystals several days after he died, something must've gone wrong."

"As I see it, there are two possible killers," Kurt said. "The person who sent the crystals or the shift supervisor who received them."

"I don't see it that way at all," Jill said. "We only know of three people in this smuggling ring, but whoever sent the crystals to the refuse tray got them from somewhere. Also, that particular robot couldn't identify galzium. Someone changed its code. The supervisor who received the crystals gave them to someone else. It's not easy to exchange controlled crystals for credits. There must be a dozen or so people mixed up in this."

"Hmm..." Izzy said with a thoughtful expression. "The IPS's investigation will definitely cover the three people we know of, but I don't think they have enough information."

"So, we might never find out who murdered Gary," Jill said with a sigh. "I sort of feel sorry for him."

After breakfast, Jill strolled to the floating train with several other commuters. Wearing her uniform and preparing for another long day, she wondered if she'd get Gary's rounds again or if Angela would assign them to someone else. It was the second day of the week, but a smile crept across her face. She usually stopped hat-ing her job after the first day and didn't even mind if Angela asked her to do Gary's rounds again.

The floating train arrived at Spencer Industries, and she filed out with the other workers. Taking the crowded antigrav lift to her office floor, she was the only one who stepped out on that level. She walked through the lobby and passed Angela's office.

"Jill," Angela called. "Would you step into my office?"

Jill expected to pick up Gary's rotation again, but she didn't mind. A lightness filled her chest; she felt safe because she met with the IPS, yesterday. She took a couple of steps past Angela's door and stopped.

"Please come in and sit," Angela said with a frown.

A sinking feeling formed in the pit of Jill's stomach as the door closed behind her.

"Good morning," Jill said, trying to break the tension.

"I've been in a series of meetings since yesterday afternoon," Angela said with a heavy sigh. "Why didn't you come to me first?"

"Uhmm..." Jill said, shifting uncomfortably in her seat. "I suppose this is about the galzium?"

"You should've told me first," Angela said with an edge in her voice. "You made me look like an idiot. I was completely blindsided when Henry Stone, the owner of the entire corporation, contacted me. I didn't know anything."

She relaxed a little as Angela seemed more upset about her reputation.

"Would you tell me what happened yesterday?" Angela asked, rubbing her temple.

Jill explained finding the galzium, realizing she wasn't safe at work, and going to the IPS. She left out Izzy's and Kurt's involvement.

"I could've kept you safe, too," Angela said, pursing her lips.

Raising a questioning eyebrow, Jill kept her mouth closed.

"Okay..." Angela said with a slow exhale. "I couldn't have kept you that safe. But you made me a laughingstock."

"Gary's dead," Jill said matter-of-factly. "He was Askovian and from a prominent Askov family. My family has no political clout, and I have no abilities. If someone was bold enough to murder Gary, they'd have no problem killing me."

Angela stared at her, nonplussed.

The silence lasted for several moments until Angela shifted closer to her desk and rubbed her face.

"What was the result of all those meetings?" Jill asked, her chest tightening.

"You're on paid suspension," Angela said in a level voice. "I have to warn you, the company almost never reverses suspensions. They only do it this way to minimize negative PR."

Jill took a few seconds to breathe deeply. She expected backlash from Spencer, but she thought it would come in a few days or even weeks. Taking for granted everyone would understand that she wasn't safe, she assumed she'd receive a reprimand.

"I'm going to need your uniform," Angela said. "You can't go back to your desk. If you have anything personal, I'll get it for you. When you're ready, a guard will escort you out of the building."

"You need me to take it off now?" Jill asked, blinking in surprise.

"I'm afraid so," Angela said in her professional company voice.

Jill stood and, with trembling fingers, unzipped her one-piece red and white uniform. Underneath, she wore a blue and yellow shirt and black pants. A moment later, she handed her overalls to Angela, still struggling to process her shock.

"What do you want from your desk?" Angela asked, climbing to her feet.

"Nothing," Jill said in a quiet voice. She'd been careful not to bring anything personal to work. She didn't want to settle into this job. At the same time, she had planned to work for a few more years. She needed to start looking for a new job soon.

A knock on the door interrupted her thoughts.

"Come," Angela said, turning to the door.

A uniformed security guard in a red and white jumpsuit that mimicked the IPS's uniform strode into the office.

"Ms. Solis, please come with me," he said, stepping to the side to give her room to pass.

Jill stuffed her shaking hands in her pockets and walked ahead of the guard. Minnie and Leo stood and watched her go, but they said nothing. A moment later, Jill exited the building, heading for the train back to the Colburns' early for the second day in a row.

When Jill walked through the door of Kurt and Izzy's apartment, they sat around the dining room table with the dampers activated, holding a silent conversation with someone. Izzy raised a finger to her lips, and Jill nodded, taking a seat on the sofa. Several minutes later, they joined her.

"I suppose you've been fired?" Izzy asked in a gentle voice.

"I'm so surprised at how fast things are moving," Jill said. "I mean, I knew the higher-ups wouldn't be happy I went to the IPS, but a suspension? The day after?"

"They're in full damage control mode," Kurt said. "Based on your statement alone, it's clear there's a smuggling ring embedded in Spencer Industries. It's possible the managers didn't know about it, which makes them look bad."

"That's all Angela kept talking about," Jill said, scoffing. "How bad I made her look. They seemed a lot less interested in the danger."

"Would you like one of my chef's specials?" Kurt asked with a grin.

"Maybe later," Jill said with a half-smile. "I wish I could go back home."

"Funny you should bring that up," Izzy said, squeezing Jill's hand. "When you walked in, we were talking to a friend who can fix your home's AI. He has run a remote diagnostic, and there's a deeply entrenched virus in every level of the AI's processing framework. But he thinks it's fixable and won't require new hardware."

"New hardware?" Jill asked with raised eyebrows. "For a virus?"

"Yes," Kurt said. "Sometimes the intruders install a small device that keeps releasing new versions of the virus. He still needs to physically check your AI, but he's confident there's only the virus."

"What about alerting the smugglers?" Jill asked.

"Enough time's gone by," Izzy said. "It's reasonable to make corrections to the AI."

"When can he start?" Jill asked with a broad grin.

"This afternoon after work," Izzy said. "He has to take your AI back to its factory settings. You'll lose any personal information it's storing for you."

"That's not a problem," Jill said. "Dad was pretty insistent on regular backups in various physical locations. The AI has nothing I can't replace."

"Excellent," Kurt said. "I'll let him know." He activated a floating screen and sent a quick message.

"I can't wait to finish my latest piece," Jill said as the weight of losing her job slightly lifted.

Later that afternoon, Izzy stepped to the front door of Jill's home, which slid open immediately.

"Ugh! It should never do that," Jill said, grimacing.

Kurt grumbled something under his breath.

"At least it's a safe neighborhood," Jill said, pursing her lips as she turned to Izzy and Kurt.

"Let me go in first," Kurt said. "I don't think anyone's in there, but just in case." He stepped around Izzy and Jill and entered the house. After a quick scan, he walked to the bedrooms in the back.

"Well, at least everything looks the same," Jill said, making her way to the still blank floating screen. She tried again to turn it off, making it disappear. Then she turned it on, but when it reappeared, it remained unresponsive.

"Hello," a tall man with bushy brown curls called out.

"Foster!" Izzy said with a quick hug. "You're just in time."

"Hello," Jill said, exchanging nods.

"Foster," Kurt said, emerging from the bedroom and giving him a tough-guy hug. "It's been a while."

"Yeah, too long," Foster said, grinning. "I don't have much time, and I need to start the process."

"The AI lives here," Kurt said, pointing at a spot in the ceiling between the living room and bathroom.

"Okay," Foster said, placing a heavy blue bag on the floor and pulling out several gadgets. The first one looked similar to the handheld scanner Jill used at work, only larger. It emitted a thin blue light that performed a search pattern before settling at a small angle away from its starting point.

"Found it," Foster said, opening a floating screen over his comm bracelet. He adjusted the window's size, adding significantly more rows of numbers and status buttons. "First, your AI's CPU is clean—I mean, physically, there are no extra pieces of hardware. The problem lies here." He pointed to something on the floating screen.

Suddenly, her comm bracelet chimed, making her jump; she'd become engrossed in Foster's work.

"It's Minnie," Jill said in a quiet voice to Izzy.

"Take it," Izzy said. "See if you can find out more about the company and the galzium."

Jill refused the vidchat but sent a message instead. It contained a casual greeting, asking what Minnie wanted.

Minnie immediately invited her over to Leo's and promised Angela wouldn't be there.

Jill chuckled, agreeing to meet. She didn't care if Angela was there or not. She was just doing her job.

CHAPTER 12

Early in the evening, Jill made her way to Leo and Roman's house. Although Mars's gravity was only forty percent of Earth's, its days were a similar length, twenty-five hours. At this time of day, her coworkers would've been off work for four or five hours. Jill reached the front door and waited for a moment.

"Leo is waiting for you in the living room," the home's AI said in a crisp voice. "Please follow the lighting in the floor."

They must have fixed their AI, she thought. *But I don't remember it being broken.*

She turned the corner, entering the old-fashioned room with its heavy decor. Minnie curled up on the sofa, and Leo chose a chair on the other side of the coffee table. Roman reclined in a chair next to him, chewing on something that turned his lips green.

Leo and Minnie stood when she entered, but Roman shoved empty bags of treats into the recycling bin.

"How are you?" Minnie asked, stepping to her side and giving her a warm hug. Jill froze for a moment, still surprised by the embrace, but she relaxed and squeezed Minnie, too.

"I'm fine now," Jill said, taking in the rest of the room. She exchanged nods with Leo and Roman.

"Good." Minnie visibly relaxed and guided her to the sofa. "Angela refused to explain why she let you go." She looked up at Jill expectantly. "You don't have to explain if you don't want to."

So, *they only invited me here for gossip*, she thought.

"We've guessed it had something to do with the news reports," Leo said. "They've been running all day."

The three of them peered at her, clearly waiting for her to elaborate.

Jill shared an abbreviated version of yesterday's events. The IPS hadn't told her not to talk to her friends. Also, she believed they'd all be safer if more people knew the truth.

"Do you know who teleported the crystals?" Roman asked, sitting up in his chair now.

"No, and I didn't stick around to find out," Jill said, frowning and reliving the moment she realized she was in danger. "What I want to know is the supervisor's name who would've received the crystals if I'd placed them in the collection slot."

Minnie and Leo exchanged glances.

"Yesterday and today, it was Betty," Leo said. "But only because she was covering for Danica."

"What happened to Danica?" Jill asked as she felt a familiar tightness forming in her chest. She knew both Betty and Danica from office parties. Betty was a plain, no-nonsense woman in her forties. Danica was a stunning, augmented brunette with green eyes. She was in her early twenties but seemed to know how to command a room. When she arrived at the last holiday party, the conversation quieted for a moment as every male head in the room turned.

"That's the problem," Minnie said. "Nobody can find her. Angela's been sending messages for about a week, but there doesn't seem to be a trace of her."

"Why would the smugglers kill her?" Jill asked with wrinkled brows. "Was she trying to steal the crystals?"

"Nobody knows, yet," Roman said, leaning forward with his elbows resting on his knees. "I've been looking through the Net, but it doesn't seem like the IPS has found anything."

"Wait, are you saying Danica disappeared the same day Gary died?" Jill asked, wide-eyed.

"Exactly," Minnie said. "The news report came out a few hours ago. It explained the IPS has been looking for Danica for the past ten days, but they're now asking for any information from the public."

"I noticed the IPS is being very transparent about this investigation," Roman said.

"Yeah, they don't want a repeat of last time," Leo said, exhaling and sinking back into his chair.

"What about Gary's latest girlfriend?" Jill asked. "Has she been around?"

"None of us have seen her since Gary..." Minnie said, clearing her throat.

A silent moment passed, and for once, Roman wasn't eating anything.

"What do you plan to do now?" Minnie asked.

"Look for the killer, of course," Jill said, crossing her arms. "This smuggling gang has completely disrupted my life, and I'm going to do something about it."

"Did you miss the part about one dead and one missing person?" Roman asked with a raised eyebrow.

"Of course not," Jill said. "I don't want to die. I'm just going to poke around and, if I find anything, turn it over to the IPS."

Minnie widened her eyes, and Leo raised his eyebrows. Roman shook his head.

"What was Gary's girlfriend's name?" Jill asked, turning to Roman.

"Faye Overton," Roman said. "But I already looked into her and found very little."

Kurt and Izzy didn't find much either, she thought. *Who is she?*

"So, we have three leads," Jill said. "Danica, Faye, and the clues from the break-ins."

"I've already looked into all three and found nothing," Roman said. "Danica's disappeared, Faye is unreachable, and the virus in our AI couldn't be removed. The service company had never seen anything like it. We had to pay for a whole new system and upgrade security."

"Mom and Dad are furious," Leo said, blowing out a breath.

"Wait. Replace everything?" Jill asked. "Why?"

"They attached some sort of hardware to the AI's CPU," Leo said. "It couldn't be removed without causing a lot of damage, which meant the AI couldn't be reset. It's been a fun few days." He added the last part sarcastically.

"What about you?" Jill asked, turning to Minnie.

"Same," Minnie said, frowning. "Only my parents screamed at me for fifteen minutes before authorizing the company to replace our system."

"Do you know what happened to Angela's AI?" Jill asked.

"It was the same," Roman said. "We all used the same company to purchase a new system."

"Didn't the complex cover her costs?" Jill asked.

"No," Minnie said. "In fact, they threatened to sue her if she didn't get it addressed immediately. Something about her nonworking system putting everyone else at risk. I didn't understand their logic, but she paid to have the work done."

Why didn't the smugglers do the same to my AI? she thought. *I didn't need to change any hardware.*

"What do you think we should do?" Leo asked skeptically.

"Could you find out more about the miners?" Jill asked. "I know that's a broad request. But who do you think would've made friends with Gary?"

"A tall blonde or brunette with long legs," Minnie said sarcastically.

Leo and Roman smirked.

"He definitely had a type," Jill said with a small smile. "I need to get going. Are you all free on the weekend?"

The three of them nodded, and Jill left shortly afterward, thinking of the questions she'd discuss with Izzy and Kurt.

Later that evening, after dinner, Jill sat in one of the overstuffed chairs facing the sofa next to Kurt. Izzy reclined on the sofa with a floating screen overhead.

"I want to move back to my house tomorrow," Jill said, eyeing Kurt and Izzy. "I feel like I'm drifting without a mooring. Someone broke into my house, and I hate that there was nothing I could've done to prevent it."

"You feel vulnerable," Izzy said, pushing the floating window away and turning to Jill. "I think you should move back, but with some precautions."

"Foster's detailed scan will finish sometime in the middle of the night," Kurt said. "He's not expecting any other surprises, but he's left a security scanner that'll detect unauthorized movement and alert you and us. It'll help with any future break-ins."

"Not that I'm being paranoid," Jill said, tilting her head. "But what does the scanner report if it's just me moving around my home?"

"Nothing," Izzy said, chuckling and pulling the floating screen closer. "If there's movement in the house, and it's you, the scanner does nothing. But if there's movement when you're not there, your comm bracelet will chime, as well as ours." She began scrolling through something on the window.

"That's what should've happened with the original AI," Jill said, setting her mouth in a straight line. "I wish I knew how they disabled it."

"Foster didn't really have any ideas," Kurt said, shrugging a shoulder and turning to Izzy.

"I think Foster has a lot of ideas," Izzy said absently. "He just doesn't always tell us."

"On a different note," Jill said, taking a sip of hot tea. "Have you found anything about Danica?"

"No," Izzy said. "It turns out Harris has been looking for her, but he kept it quiet. Otherwise, our contacts at the IPS would've let us know."

"Do you think Harris knows about your contacts?" Jill asked.

"He probably knows someone's leaking information," Kurt said, "but doesn't know exactly who."

"I've found a little more about Faye, though," Izzy said, her eyes narrowing at something on the screen. "She's married, her husband is part of the Pendleton family, and she's a Reader."

"Did you say married?" Jill asked with raised eyebrows.

"Yup," Izzy said with a smirk. "Was she dating Gary? Was she really just friends with Gary's sister? Makes you wonder." She turned her screen so that Kurt and Jill could see it. Faye had long, jet-black, wavy hair, a perfectly symmetrical face, and stormy gray eyes.

"Did he only date augments?" Kurt asked with a hint of disgust.

"How can we find out more about her connection to Gary?" Jill asked, placing her empty cup on the side table next to her.

"Want more?" Kurt asked, swallowing the last of his tea.

"Not now," Jill said, letting ideas flow through her mind. "What if we just ask her?"

"No!" Kurt and Izzy said at the same time.

"That's the fastest way to put a target on your back," Izzy said, setting her lips in a grim line. "She could've been cheating on her husband, or she was Gary's contact for the galzium."

"I wasn't going to ask her directly," Jill said, blinking several times in surprise at their reaction. "I was going to be clever about it. For example, what if I invited everyone from work to a quiet get-together and invited Faye, her husband, and Ellie?"

"I see," Izzy said. "Even their responses to your invitation would tell you a lot about how close they were to Gary."

"Exactly," Jill said as her shoulders relaxed. "The only thing is, I'm not sure what to do about Danica since nobody can find her."

"We'll stay in contact with our friends in the IPS," Kurt said, munching on a cinnamon sugar cookie. "Do you want one?"

Jill shook her head.

Izzy giggled. "I thought you said you were full."

"I was a minute ago," Kurt said, stumbling slightly over his words. "But I baked them earlier today, and I wouldn't want them to go to waste."

"I've been wondering about the break-ins," Jill said. "It's strange the smugglers treated my house differently from everyone else's. It could be they knew I wasn't that close to Gary, or they thought I didn't have a good place to hide the galzium."

"Do you think that's important?" Izzy asked.

"Somehow, I sense it is," Jill said, staring at the ceiling for a moment. "It feels like that difference is telling me something."

"It could be telling you one of your coworkers lied," Kurt said, drawing his eyebrows together.

"Yes, it's something like that," Jill said. "Can your friends at IPS check on the actual work done in their homes?"

Izzy exhaled slowly.

"That'd be difficult," Kurt said. "Our friends can access peripheral information that Harris doesn't mind sharing, but involving themselves in an active investigation could get them fired."

"Oh..." Jill said in a quiet voice. "I'll think of something else."

"How do you plan to meet Ellie in a couple of days?" Izzy asked, pushing the floating window toward the back of the sofa.

"I'm going to the disembarkation dock," Jill said and immediately raised both hands. "Let me finish. I want to see who comes to greet her. Angela is the only family I know of."

"We'll come with you," Kurt said. "If there's a smuggling ring, they may be watching you."

"Jill, I wish you'd stay home," Izzy said, concern in her voice.

"But that's the problem with this whole thing," Jill said in a raised voice. "They broke into my house and rearranged my belongings on purpose. They're trying to intimidate me, and I'm not backing down. If I hide away, I'll be too afraid to do anything. I just can't allow them to do that to me."

CHAPTER 13

Early the following morning, Kurt and Izzy helped Jill move back to her house. They helped her reset the home's AI and waited until she had activated the special floating art screen she used for her projects.

"I think that's everything," Jill said with a broad grin as she flopped onto her sofa. "It feels so good to be back home."

"What are you going to do first?" Izzy asked, settling into a chair opposite.

"I'm going to add the finishing touches to the waves in my digital painting," Jill said and paused, quickly scanning her living room. "Is it okay to talk here?"

"Of course," Izzy said, her eyebrows knitting. "What are you thinking about?"

"In your home, you use dampers for important conversations," Jill said. "Should I do that too?"

"No," Izzy said, laughing. "We mainly use those things to protect our friends. Foster and the others have secure jobs with the IPS, and they don't want to jeopardize them. Also, someone at the IPS periodically surveils us even though we haven't been involved with them for years. It takes us a few days to find the equipment."

"We've just completed a sweep here," Kurt said with a small smile. "You can say whatever you want."

"I want to start trying to crack the puzzle safe," Jill said. "Verifying Gary's last words would make me feel a little safer. I probably won't get very far, but I want to give it a try."

Jill's comm bracelet chimed, interrupting their conversation.

After pressing a button on her comm, Minnie's frowning face filled the floating screen.

"Minnie, what's wrong?" Jill asked, sitting up straighter.

"Gary's sister was just here," Minnie said in a wobbly voice. "She invited all of us to Gary's private memorial service tomorrow."

"Wait, did you say Gary's sister?" Jill asked, wide-eyed.

"Yeah. I've only met her once, but she looks like a pretty version of Gary," Minnie said with a sad chuckle.

"What's her name?" Jill asked, trying to get more confirmation.

"Eloise Turner, but everyone calls her Ellie," Minnie said. "Please say you'll come. You worked with Gary, too. You're practically family."

"Is this a special work-place service?" Jill asked. "Are you sure it's okay?"

"It's a private funeral," Minnie said, wiping her eyes. "She apologized for not letting us know sooner. It took her a while to reach Angela and get our contact information." In Askov society, it was common for prominent families to have two funerals: one for just family and another for the rest of society. The second funeral usually turned into a platform to display their wealth or power.

"Will there be a public funeral?" Jill asked.

"It didn't sound like it," Minnie said. "They barely organized the private one. Very few of Gary's relatives even liked him."

"Ah, I see," Jill said.

"Look, I'm sorry," Minnie said, glancing at something off-screen. "I have to go, but I'll send the time and location of the memorial service."

"Of course, see you tomorrow," Jill said, and the screen went dark.

"I was wondering how to meet Ellie," Jill said with a lopsided smile. "But the Turner family has solved that problem for me." She turned to Izzy and Kurt. "There's a funeral tomorrow, and now I'm thinking up ways to steer the conversation. I really hope Faye will be there."

"Should we come with you?" Kurt asked, his face twisting in a comical expression. "You know... to keep you safe."

"I'm sure I'll be fine in such a public space," Jill said with a soft chuckle.

A few minutes later, Jill and Kurt sat cross-legged on the floor of the guest room. They'd pushed the guest bed against the far wall, where Izzy reclined, scrolling through the Net, looking for instructions on how to open a puzzle safe. Even though Kurt and Izzy assured her she was safe in her home, her shoulders tightened as she looked at the floor. Then she gave herself a mental shake and began.

Jill carefully examined the perfectly smooth beige carpet with no seams. This was one of her dad's trapdoor contraptions that left the carpet looking and feeling uniform. It was probably the main reason the smugglers never found her safe. Using her comm bracelet, she activated a floating screen that displayed the safe's control panel.

"I only saw your dad open this safe a handful of times," Kurt said. "Pax was very private. I'm amazed at the amount of work he put into it."

A small smile crept across her face; she liked hearing stories about her dad. Selecting the open button caused an outline of a square meter to appear on the carpet. Then the square sank a few centimeters into the floor and slid completely out of the way underneath the floor, supporting her and Kurt. She swiped her hand over a DNA reader, and the door dematerialized.

"That's my favorite part of opening the safe." Jill grinned.

Gary's tan puzzle box sat on top and so did the tracking armor.

"Mind if I take a look?" Kurt asked, and she placed the box in his hands. He ran his hands over its textured surface, which was covered with tiny triangles set at odd angles. "It has a sharp, bumpy feeling all over."

"Yeah, most are like that," Jill said. "The texture hides the locking mechanism." She reached into the safe and pulled out the armor. "Gary was wearing this when he visited and gave it to me. But I'm not sure why he left it for me."

"He already knew he was in trouble," Izzy said with a slight frown. "I think he wanted to keep you safe."

"More like he wanted to make sure I delivered Ellie's necklace," Jill said sarcastically.

"Are you even sure it's a necklace?" Izzy asked.

"No," Jill said with a pinched face. "He lied about a lot of things when he visited. That's the main reason I want to open this."

She turned the armor over in her hand.

"Let me see," Izzy said, reaching for the thin, curved device. After Jill handed it to her, she scrutinized it for a few seconds. "It's fairly high quality. I wonder where he got it."

"Yeah, I can see from here," Kurt said, gazing at the device. "I'm tempted to think he stole it. Even the lower-quality armors are unbelievably expensive."

"Unless you work for the IPS," Izzy said, smirking.

Carefully sifting through her parents' belongings, Jill eventually found what she was looking for. She chuckled softly and nudged her dad's tool bag out of the safe.

"I think I've seen that bag a hundred times," Kurt said with a wistful smile. "When we were in our teens, Pax fell in with the wrong crowd. Nothing I could say would change his mind as he assisted a gang with robbing a few museums." He chuckled, shaking his head. "You might be wondering what a bunch of adults were doing with a teenager, but Pax was really talented."

Jill had heard this story a hundred times before, but it was one of her favorites.

"During their last heist, a guard showed up unexpectedly," Kurt said with a chortle. "That probably saved his life. You see, Pax was always a little heavy. Unable to run as fast as the others, the guard caught him. The only thing that reduced his long sentence was his age. He also cooperated and told them everything he knew about the gang. But—" Kurt paused for dramatic effect. "As it turned out, he never learned anything about their operation. The gang compartmentalized every aspect of their business. Pax never knew their real names, where they lived, how they learned about the items they stole, or what they did with the loot. Nothing."

The three of them laughed at Kurt's story.

"Dad taught me everything he knew about safe-cracking," Jill said with a sad smile. "Even though I loved learning, I was just never as accurate or as fast." She reached into the bag and pulled out the puzzle scanner. It was specifically designed to peer into the depths of a safe, creating a multilayered road map. But there were no signs on this map, meaning the person had to rely on their intuition. Taking the safe from Kurt, she placed it on the floor between them. She held the scanner over Gary's puzzle box for several seconds until it chimed.

"Finally," Jill said with a half-smile. She quickly placed the scanner beside the puzzle safe and opened a second floating window to view the scanner's map. She frowned and then sighed. "I've never seen anything this complicated."

"That looks like a bowl of spaghetti," Kurt said, chuckling.

"Now, don't interrupt her," Izzy said absently from the bed. "But, Jill, if you get stuck, I've found a few sets of instructions."

"Okay," Jill said as her eyes swept over the floating map. After several minutes, she finally noticed three inline indentations. "Isn't that the end of the puzzle?" Her eyes followed a thin line that trailed away from the three depressions. It took a circuitous route across the inner workings of the puzzle safe. She traced it around subtle blinking lights, tiny metal structures, and more randomly placed dents.

When the thin line reached the middle of the map, it circled two tiny dents. Jill chuckled. "This is it." She turned her gaze to the puzzle box and finally noticed the very shallow dimples. "Wow, they're so shallow. How was anyone supposed to see that?"

Using two fingers, she gently placed them in the dents. Immediately, the safe whirred to life, and she felt the vibrations as the complicated locking system activated. "It's working."

Kurt and Izzy clapped softly.

Unfortunately, several seconds later, the movement stopped.

"What?" Jill said, turning back to the map. Finally she noticed something she hadn't seen before.

"Oh no," Jill said, tightening her jaw. "Someone turned this box into a DNA lock. That's why it was so complicated." She turned the puzzle safe's map to Kurt and Izzy. "Buried deep in one of the map's levels, I found the alterations. If it's forced open, the box will probably destroy the contents." She glared at the safe with pursed lips.

"Who takes the time to modify a puzzle box?" Kurt asked, frowning.

"Someone trying to smuggle contraband or protect jewelry?" Izzy asked with a raised brow.

"Do you think I should hand this over to the IPS or Ellie?" Jill asked.

"The only safe option is to hand this over to the IPS," Izzy said. "We can do it the same way we did with the galzium."

"I'm afraid I have to agree with Izzy," Kurt said. "This is way too dangerous."

"Well, in any case, I still want to visit when the Atlas docks tomorrow," Jill said. "Ellie won't be there, but Gary wanted me to be there for a reason."

"We'll go with you," Izzy said, turning to Kurt, who nodded.

I wonder who I'm supposed to meet? Jill thought.

Later that afternoon, Jill started a vidchat with Veronica, the owner of the Red Frame Gallery.

"Do you have a date that doesn't conflict with other artists?" Jill asked, adding notes to a second floating screen.

"Yes, but I have a few questions," Veronica said. "How extravagant do you want to go? We could host a full dinner or just snacks."

"Maybe fancy hors d'oeuvres," Jill said, quickly adding more notes. "Something small and sweet."

"I have the perfect caterer," Veronica said giggling. "You'll love him."

"Care to share?" Jill said with a lopsided grin.

"It's a surprise, but one you'll love," Veronica said, turning to something off-screen.

"Okay," Jill said. "Also, I want to display all four of my Earthscape images, but I worry there won't be enough room for the visual memoirs."

"Let me handle that," Veronica said, moving her hands on something out of Jill's view.

Their conversation continued for several more minutes. A comfortable peace settled deep inside Jill as she took her first real steps toward her dream.

CHAPTER 14

The next afternoon, Jill arrived at the Anteros Memorial Center. It was a two-story white building with arches over the windows and columns framing the entrance. The design was modern but hinted at a past religion that very few Askovs still believed in. The center stood on the edge of Anteros, and she glanced through the city's clear dome at the orange, rugged landscape as she approached from the floating train.

Jill checked her dark gray dress and took a deep breath before stepping toward the front double doors, which slid open automatically.

"May I help you?" a tall man with gray hair asked, wearing a formal black jumpsuit. It was a quiet space with heavy, dark red carpet and old-fashioned floral prints in gold-colored frames.

"I'm here for Gary Turner's service," Jill said, adjusting a silver clasp holding her hair in a ponytail on her neck.

"Right this way," the man said, gesturing to another set of faux wood double doors.

"Jill," Minnie said in a somber voice with red-rimmed eyes. "I'm so glad you could make it." She turned to the woman with platinum blonde hair and crystal blue eyes. "This is Gary's sister, Ellie Turner."

"I'm happy to meet some of my brother's friends," Ellie said with a small smile. "I didn't realize Gary had so many. Sorry, this was all organized last-minute."

Jill tried not to stare at the resemblance between brother and sister. But where Gary's face had been all angles and hard edges, hers was soft and heart-shaped. Minnie's description, calling her pretty, was accurate.

"It's nice to meet you," Jill said. She noted that Minnie seemed more upset than Ellie, but everyone experienced grief differently.

"Ellie, we need your help with something," an older platinum-haired woman called.

"That's Aunt Lily. Excuse me," Ellie said, turning and hurrying away.

"Come." Minnie linked arms with Jill and gently led her to their coworkers.

Angela stiffened when Jill arrived and muttered a greeting, refusing to meet her eyes.

"Glad you could make it," Leo said with a strained expression. "I think we're the only friends Gary had."

"We only gamed about once a week—I feel a little like a fraud being here," Jill shifted uncomfortably from foot to foot. "The rest of you were really his friends."

"I think it's just fine," Minnie said. "We all worked together or hung out with him."

"We probably knew Gary better than his family," Roman said, glancing at the group of mostly platinum-haired family members.

"Are they really all augments?" Jill asked. "I'm not judging. It's just such an expensive procedure. I didn't realize the Turners had that much wealth."

"The Turners are closely related to the Stones," Roman said with a smirk. "The head of Spencer Industries is now a Stone. They're just as wealthy as the Spencers."

Jill reflected on that for a moment.

"Have you two met?" Ellie said, breaking into the quiet and gesturing to a stunning, tall woman with jet-black hair. "Faye, this is Jill."

The two exchanged nods.

"This is my husband, Vance," Faye said, gesturing to a tall, heavyset, red-headed man. His facial features gave him away as a Pendleton.

"Oh, are you family, too?" Jill asked, suspecting that was not the case. But she was afraid she might not get a better chance to talk to the woman who could've been Gary's girlfriend.

"No, we did business together," Vance said, examining Jill for the first time.

"I think everybody's here," Ellie said, turning to a person in an all-black suit who'd just entered. "It's the organizer. Let's get started."

Jill scanned the crowd, mostly filled with relatives. Faye and Vance joined Ellie and sat with the Turner family.

Sitting with her former coworkers, Jill chose a seat between Angela and Minnie. Angela occasionally wiped her eyes and hadn't said a word to her beyond a greeting.

"Which one is Ellie's husband?" Jill whispered.

"She's not married," Minnie said in a low voice.

Jill nodded at the confirmation.

Her ex-coworkers wore somber expressions, but Jill noticed the relatives seemed mostly bored. Even Ellie kept up a quiet stream of chatter with Faye during the entire ceremony.

The officiant stood at a lectern, arranging something on a floating screen, and began the service.

"We're gathered here today to reflect on the remarkable life of Gareth Turner," the officiant said. He droned on with general information that could have applied to any deceased person.

Gary's relatives stifled yawns, fidgeted in their seats, and muttered to each other throughout the officiant's speech.

He must have done some terrible things to cause such a break with the family, Jill thought. *But then, what was really in the puzzle safe? He'd lied about Ellie arriving on the Atlas and her marriage; what else had he lied about?*

After the service, everyone stepped to the next room for refreshments. Jill, Minnie, Leo, and Roman stood together, chatting about work.

"I see Angela left early," Roman said with a smirk. "I think she's uncomfortable around Jill."

"No," Minnie said around a mouthful of a cheesy quiche square. "Gary's passing hit her hard. She hasn't really been the same since."

Leo turned to Minnie for a moment.

"How has she changed?" Jill asked, swallowing coffee.

"I noticed more of a change after someone broke into her home," Leo said, taking a sip of wine.

"Mmm..." Roman said. "This cheese thing is good."

"I noticed she became much more withdrawn," Minnie said. "She's barely visited, yet she's always gone on the weekends. I don't think she's coping well."

"Hello," Faye said as she joined their circle. "I know I haven't met all of you, but I wanted to say how terribly sorry I am for your loss."

Leo and Roman nodded.

"Thank you," Minnie said in a wobbly voice. "I still can't believe he's gone."

Leo wrapped a protective arm around her.

"We appreciate your condolences," Jill said, peering at the group. "Uhmm... you said you were in business with Gary. Was that related to a casino?"

"Something like that," Faye said, her smile frozen.

"Sweetheart," Vance said, cupping Faye's elbow and guiding her away. "Some of the family asked for you."

Jill studied their retreating backs as they headed directly toward the door leading out of the center.

"I think you rattled them," Roman said with a raised eyebrow.

"Yeah," Minnie said. "I'm not sure how smart that was. I didn't know until today that they were business partners. We all assumed they were dating."

"If their business had to do with Gary's gambling," Leo said, "they could be dangerous."

"Do you think the people who broke into our homes would kill Gary and then come to his funeral?" Roman asked in a loud whisper.

"Keep your voice down," Leo said, an edge in his voice. "I don't think Faye or Vance are the problem; it's their contacts I'm worried about."

Roman shrugged a shoulder.

Jill studied Ellie, who chuckled with some family members as if they were attending a reunion instead of a memorial service. She began

to wonder whom she'd meet at the disembarkation terminal.

Three hours after the memorial service, Jill,
Izzy, and Kurt reached the receiving terminal for passengers disembarking from the Atlas
Starship. The first mini-shuttle descended from
the sky. A moment later, a flood of about five
hundred passengers spilled through the open
side doors. The entire platform turned into a
sea of bodies, creating a cacophony of crying
babies, screeching moms trying to manage the
chaos, and loud male voices calling to friends
and family.

Jill surveyed the crowd, trying to focus on
platinum blond hair. What she hadn't accounted
for was the sea of heads covered in light-col-
ored scarves, hats, jacket hoods, and one bright,
sparkling cap.

"Do you see anything?" Jill asked with
scrunched eyebrows.

"Lots of people," Izzy said, holding a scanner.
It wasn't like the ones Jill had used at work; instead, it was from the IPS. It allowed the holder

to instantly scour a crowd, looking for a particular person or a group of people.

"Just point me in the right direction," Kurt said. "I'll get to her."

"Got her," Izzy said, looking at a floating screen just over the scanner. "But she's with Faye and Vance."

"Let me see," Kurt said, squinting at the window. "That's interesting. I say we hold off on approaching and just monitor them."

"What are they doing?" Jill asked, still focused on the mass of bodies. "I can't see a thing."

"Just standing and looking around," Izzy said.

"Like they're waiting for somebody?" Jill asked. "I wonder if that's who I would've met, if I'd followed Gary's instructions. But... how would they know to meet me? What was Gary's plan?"

"Is anyone else standing still?" Kurt asked, turning to the thinning crowd.

Izzy took a moment to sweep the scanner over the entire crowd. "A few others are standing around, but they're guards. Maybe IPS? Not sure."

After about an hour, the dock cleared. Ellie, Faye, and Vance had left thirty minutes earlier. Now, Izzy scanned a few stragglers.

"Where do you think Ellie, Faye, and Vance went?" Jill asked. "Maybe we should've followed them."

"No. Harris was not far behind the group," Izzy said, setting her lips in a straight line.

"Did Gary send me here to pass the puzzle safe to the thieves?" Jill asked, frowning. "Does that mean Ellie, Faye, and Vance are the smugglers? Everything he talked about and wrote was a lie!"

"Excuse me," Agent Rogers said, standing directly behind the group. The setting sun caught her red, orange hair.

Jill jumped, Izzy lowered the scanner, and Kurt slowly spun on his heel.

"Mr. and Ms. Colburn," Agent Rogers said, her face placid. "Ms. Solis. How are you this evening?"

Jill, Izzy, and Kurt gazed at her freckled face, nonplussed.

"Would the three of you please follow me?" Rogers asked, gesturing to the large, two-story building next to the Atlas's shuttle.

"I don't know," Jill said hesitantly.

"Dear, I think it wouldn't hurt to hear what they have to say," Izzy said with a reassuring smile.

"We'll be with you every step of the way," Kurt said.

The three of them followed Rogers into the building. Jill wondered if she should explain her interaction with Gary. Would she be in trouble with the IPS? Would the smugglers come after her?

They entered the building on the ground floor, and Jill gasped. The floor looked like a giant warehouse filled with organized containers. But the sight that caused her to freeze was an open container with Danica's body lying beside it.

CHAPTER 15

D anica was a stunning woman with flaw-less skin and wavy, light-brown hair. Even now, with a blanket covering most of her body, she looked as if she'd only fallen asleep. Jill remained frozen, unable to process the scene in front of her. Uniformed IPS agents filled the warehouse, recording evidence and talking quietly with each other.

"We can't stay here," Rogers said. "Follow me." She led the way to an antigrav lift, and they took it to the second floor.

The image of Danica lying lifeless on the floor kept running through Jill's mind. *Who'd killed her? Why her? Am I next?* She looked at Izzy, unsure of what to say. But Izzy grasped her hand and gave it a reassuring squeeze.

As the three of them made it out of the lift, Ellie, Faye, Vance, and a well-dressed man stepped in. It took Jill a moment to register who they were as they crossed paths; her mind was still on Danica.

Vance and the well-dressed man continued their conversation. Ellie hung on every word, wide-eyed and nodding frequently. But Faye eyed Jill closely as the doors closed.

"I'm guessing Ellie Turner and the Overtons are leaving with their attorney," Kurt said in a casual tone to Rogers.

"You know I can't comment," Rogers said, giving him a side-eye. "You don't work for the IPS anymore."

Kurt chuckled softly.

A moment later, they entered a conference room with a large white table, circled by gray padded chairs, and a large floating screen dominating one wall.

Harris and his boss, Agent Leigh, sat on one side, while Izzy, Kurt, and Jill sat opposite. Rogers slipped out of the room. Jill began to tremble as the realization of what had happened set in. She'd felt powerful announcing to Izzy and Kurt that she was going after the smugglers. But seeing Danica dead... she shivered. Clutching her fingers together, she tried to hide their shaking.

Agent Leigh was closer in age to the Colburns, and she began the interview by glaring at Kurt, who plastered a genial smile on his face.

"I thought I told you not to get involved in any more cases," Leigh said, an edge in her voice.

"Before we get too far into this conversation," Harris said, activating a floating screen over his comm bracelet, "do you consent to being recorded?"

They all agreed, and Harris took notes while recording their conversation.

"We've been following your orders," Izzy said in a relaxed, casual tone. "But this is a special case. We promised Jill's parents we'd always look out for her. When she got tangled up with Gary and the galzium, we had to help."

"How exactly are you involved with Mr. Turner?" Leigh asked, her eyes narrowing at Jill.

Jill hesitated, glancing at Izzy, who nodded her support. Izzy and Kurt clearly knew Agent Leigh and felt comfortable with her. But Jill simply wanted to bolt. It felt as if the danger closed in on her, and she didn't quite know whom to trust. Taking a steadying breath, she explained everything about Gary's visit two weeks ago, the puzzle safe he left with her, and the letter mailed to her after he died. She even described again the steps she took when she discovered the galzium.

"Well, at least you were honest about the galzium," Leigh said sarcastically.

"I have been honest," Jill said, her voice raised as anger washed away her fear. "I just didn't volunteer some information. Someone would happily kill me for what's in that box, and I think the only thing that saved my life was that they couldn't find it or my family's safe."

A moment of stunned silence settled over the room while Jill glared at Leigh, who pursed her lips. Kurt stifled his laughter.

"Yes, well, thank you for clearing that up," Harris said, reaching for something on the chair beside him. "Does your puzzle safe look like this?"

Jill nodded. "How did you... Is that the box mentioned in the surveillance vids?"

"Yes but this one's empty," Harris said, placing the open safe on the table. The outside looked identical to the one in Jill's safe, but she'd never seen the interior.

"Do you know what happened to the contents?" Leigh asked, narrowing her eyes.

"Of course not," Jill said, staring at the open puzzle box. "There's something I don't understand. I couldn't open the puzzle safe Gary left because it had a DNA lock. Why is this open?"

"How do you know about the DNA lock?" Harris asked, shifting his gaze from Jill to Izzy and Kurt.

"What did you tell her?" Leigh asked, glaring at Kurt.

Kurt and Izzy shrugged. Jill shifted uncomfortably in her seat.

"Maybe something went wrong, like a fight among smugglers," Jill said, trying to change the topic. "He obviously couldn't pick up the next galzium shipment. And that must have been what I intercepted at work."

Leigh and Harris exchanged a look.

"In any case, we'd like to accompany you back to your house," Harris said. "We'll retrieve the puzzle safe from your home."

Leigh's comm chimed. She opened a floating window and read a message. She turned the window to Harris, who read it and nodded before turning back to Jill.

"I just want to confirm a few things," Harris said. "Mr. Turner's letter brought you here. But you were at his memorial service earlier today and knew Ellie Turner already resided in the city. Why did you come?"

"I wanted to know why Gary sent me here," Jill said.

"It would've taken hours for all passengers to disembark," Harris said. "Only the first of four shuttles has made it to Anteros. Did you plan to wait the entire time?"

"There really wasn't a plan beyond showing up. But..."

"Yes?" Harris asked, his eyes narrowing.

"It was strange to run into Faye at the memorial service and here," Jill said, peering at the tabletop, thinking.

"Maybe she was following you?" Kurt asked.

"She knows Ellie and the Turner family well," Jill said. "Also, before the doors to the lift closed, she looked at me strangely. I don't know. There's something about her..."

Agent Harris and his boss sat silently, watching the exchange between Jill and Kurt. They waited for a moment before continuing.

"Do you know why we called you into this room?"

"I'm not even sure what this building is," Jill said, knowing he'd referred to Danica downstairs. She just couldn't bring herself to mention her first.

"You're in Anteros' largest warehouse," Harris said. "This is the main storage facility for imported and exported cargo."

"What?" Jill blinked. "Someone tried to mail Danica's body?" She squeezed her hands together tightly and stared at the table.

"Are you alright?" Izzy asked, rubbing her back. "We could continue this conversation later."

"Could I have some water?" Jill asked in a quiet voice.

Kurt quickly reached for the meal crafter, and a moment later, a tall glass of water materialized on the table.

Jill drank deeply and exhaled. She considered postponing the interview with Harris, but a frisson of fear ran down her spine, thinking of the killers.

"Dear, I think we should wait until you're feeling better," Izzy said.

"No," Jill said. "I want to tell them everything. The more people who know, the safer I'll be."

"How well did you know Danica Peters?" Harris asked, peering closely at her.

"I met her a few times at company parties," Jill said. "Otherwise, I never spent time with her."

"Wasn't she the supervisor for your rounds?" Harris asked.

"Oh, yes," Jill said, relaxing a little. "But I never saw or spoke to her during work hours. If I needed to send something, I'd put it in the slot."

"Yes, we're familiar with the process," Harris said. "Where were you on the night Gary died?"

"At home, working on my latest composition," Jill said. "I was by myself until Gary showed up with the puzzle safe."

"We don't have any record of Gary visiting you," Leigh said.

"Yeah, he used tracking armor," Jill said. "He told me about it because I complained he was putting me in danger. But he assured me no one could monitor him."

Harris grunted, taking notes, and Leigh leaned a little closer.

"Why is Danica's body in a warehouse?" Jill asked.

"We were hoping you could shed some light on that," Harris said.

"I don't know," Jill said, shaking her head. "I'm just so confused. How did she die? Who'd want to kill her?"

"It was the same as Gary, a blaster wound," Harris said. "We don't know who'd want to kill her. We've just begun our investigation."

Ideas filled Jill's mind about smugglers double-crossing each other, a thief who made the wrong decision, and innocents caught in the crossfire. *Why would someone kill Gary and Danica?*

A few hours after the interview, a troop of IPS agents escorted Jill to her house. They rode in a small, cramped hovercar, one of the few allowed within the Anteros dome. It was dark gray inside and divided into two compartments. The front had room for a driver and a passenger, where Rogers and Leigh sat. The back comprised two rows of seats, where Jill sat wedged between Izzy and Kurt while facing Harris, Swales, and one agent she didn't recognize.

A second, larger hovercar followed them, filled with more IPS agents. Periodically, Jill heard their conversations, which revolved around checking for any stray or unaccounted-for hovercraft, corruption of the onboard AI, and unusual activity around Jill's home. With all their checks cleared, they began their descent.

Both IPS hovercraft landed on the broad walkway surrounding the park. It was the closest they could land without crushing a house. The IPS agents from the second hovercraft immediately filed out into the night and spread throughout the neighborhood's lighted walkways. She lost sight of them a few minutes after they exited.

Izzy and Kurt walked beside Jill as if to protect her from an attack. They ambled along a lighted walkway, but secretly, she thought this was all overkill. The killers didn't operate in the open, at least based on everything she knew. They were more likely to strike when she was asleep—unless she handed the puzzle safe over to the IPS.

A few minutes later, Harris stepped into her house first, followed by Rogers, and a moment later, they returned.

"We've scouted all the rooms," Harris said. "It's all clear."

"Now, where is the safe?" Leigh asked.

"I don't mind handing everything over to you," Jill said. "But I can't let you look into my family's safe."

"That's unacceptable," Leigh said in a raised voice. "We're investigating two deaths. We have a right to follow clues wherever they lead."

"Come on, Leigh," Izzy said, her lips set in a straight line. "You know you need approval from a judge. Since it's so late, you'll have to wait until tomorrow."

"You don't work for the IPS anymore," Leigh said, glaring at Izzy. "I could have you thrown out right now."

"Then you'll never get that puzzle box," Jill said, pursing her lips.

Kurt chuckled quietly.

A muscle in Leigh's jaw began to twitch as she looked between Jill and Izzy. Finally, she pushed past Kurt and stormed out of the house.

Harris and Rogers watched the entire exchange quietly.

"Ms. Solis, would you retrieve the puzzle safe and the tracking armor?" Harris asked calmly.

Jill glanced at Izzy and Kurt.

"Don't worry," Kurt said with a smirk. "We won't let them leave the living room."

"Wait," Izzy said, removing something from her wrist. "It's a personal sniffer. It'll alert you if Harris or Rogers has installed surveillance equipment while they were looking around."

Harris gritted his teeth, and Rogers rolled her eyes.

Jill slipped the device onto the same arm as her comm and strolled to the back bedroom.

Several minutes later, she handed the puzzle safe, armor, and handwritten letter to Harris, who called in some of the IPS agents. After a moment's conversation, they all left.

"I'm proud of you," Kurt said with a full-bellied laugh. "Leigh can be a bully, and the worst thing you can do around her is show any weakness."

"I'm so glad this is finally over," Izzy said with a small smile.

"It really isn't," Jill said thoughtfully. "Two people are still dead, and we don't know anything about the smuggling ring. Despite handing over that box, I still don't feel safe."

CHAPTER 16

Jill fell into the kind of deep sleep that happened when she was sick or had a grueling day. Usually, she didn't remember her dreams and hardly moved during the night, waking up in the same position.

This time, she dreamed she was on an old rowboat, gently rocked by the waves. The funny thing was, she had been born and raised in Anteros. She'd never seen a boat or any large body of water. But in her dream, it all made sense anyway.

"Jill," a soothing female voice called. "Time to wake up."

From the depths of her slumber, she began a slow ascent to the surface. First, she remembered she was in her bedroom and not on a boat. Then she wondered who had spoken to her. Suddenly, her eyes popped open, and she screamed!

"Quiet," Faye said in a gentle voice. "I'm not here to hurt you. Quiet."

Jill sat bolt upright, eyeing Faye's shadowy form. A second later, the light's luminosity gradually increased but stopped before hurting her eyes. She held her blanket closely like a shield while scooting a couple of centimeters toward the headboard.

"Good morning," Faye said with a genial smile. "I'm sorry to wake you, but really, it's the middle of the morning. I thought you'd already be awake."

Jill blinked, not quite comprehending the scene in front of her.

"What... What are you doing here?" Jill asked in a croaky voice. "How did you get in?"

"I'll start with the second question," Faye said, as if holding a lecture in a classroom. "We used a military device that disables most doors. Unfortunately, I'm not allowed to tell you too much about it. But I'll add that it struggled with your AI both times we entered. You must've customized your security. It's obvious there's more to you than we originally thought, Jillian Solis."

"Military? That's how you broke in?" Jill asked, remembering some lessons from her dad. "Are you here with your husband? What do you want?"

"Would you get dressed and meet us in your living room?" Faye asked, heading toward the door. "By the way, we've disabled your comm and AI." She paused at the door, turning back to Jill. "I promise we won't hurt you." She left, and the door slid shut.

Jill relaxed her grip on the blanket, and her mind began to race. She reached for her comm and frantically tried to activate it. Nothing.

Didn't Foster say he rigged something that would detect movement in my house? she thought. *Why didn't that work?*

"Hello," Jill called, trying to access her home's AI. Using her private access code, she tried again, but the AI never responded. Realizing she was out of options, she sighed and pulled on a long-sleeved lavender shirt with black pants.

Are they going to kill me, too? she thought.

A moment later, she stepped into her living room to find Faye and her husband, Vance, reclining in two yellow chairs facing her sofa. They each held a coffee cup, while crumbs from something sat on a plate beside Vance.

"Please have a seat," Vance said, gesturing to the empty sofa.

Jill suppressed a shudder, sitting on the edge of the sofa with her back straight. It was unsettling for them to invite her to sit in her own house.

"I suppose you're wondering why we're here," Vance said, placing his empty cup and plate in the recycling.

Jill nodded.

"I'm a Reader," Faye said. "Did you know?"

"No," Jill said, shaking her head. "You read my mind?"

"When we crossed paths at the lift," Faye said with a lopsided smile.

"But I would've only been thinking about Danica," Jill said, confusion evident in her voice.

"Not quite. You were thinking about your personal investigation," Faye said with a half-smile. "That made me wonder about you. Why were you investigating Gary?"

"At the funeral, I would've been thinking about my investigation, too," Jill said, furrowing her eyebrows. "But I shielded my mind."

"I knew you wanted to talk to me and Vance," Faye said. "But I didn't realize you were conducting your investigation then."

"Also, our sources informed us you handed the puzzle safe to the IPS," Vance said, frowning. "You've caused us to change our plans twice. There's nothing we can do about it now, but where did you hide it?"

Jill stared, nonplussed. *Is he serious*?

"There's a safe in the guest room," Faye said, leaning forward.

Jill's head snapped toward Faye with a new realization. "My mind is shielded. How can you still read my thoughts?"

Faye chuckled and turned to her husband. "I can tell you how to open it if you like."

"Why didn't we detect it when we were here?" Vance asked.

"It's a defense created by her dad," Faye said, her eyes boring into Jill's. "She doesn't know much about it. Nobody does."

"Faye can read your mind even through your shield," Vance said, snickering. "Thanks for telling us about the safe; you may just have saved our lives."

"What're you talking about?" Jill asked, turning from Faye to Vance as she realized she had never felt Faye's presence in her mind.

"Let's just say..." Faye said, "some members of our group won't tolerate failure without a good explanation."

Faye's words filtered through Jill's mind.

"I assumed you were the leaders," Jill said. "But then a leader wouldn't be picking up... galzium, was it? You wouldn't do that in person. You'd hire a lackey. Was that Gary's job? Ellie's?"

"It seems you've figured some things out," Vance said, his eyebrows furrowed. "If I tell you too much, you'll be in danger."

"One more thing, about a week ago, Gary visited me here," Jill said. She explained what had happened. "After he died, he sent a physical letter urging me to meet Ellie when the Atlas arrived. But almost everything he mentioned in the letter was a lie. Ellie isn't married. You two and Ellie were at the Atlas disembarkation—she didn't arrive on the Atlas. The puzzle safe contained galzium and not jewelry. I don't understand why he told all those lies."

Faye and Vance chuckled, exchanging glances.

"Gary thought he was some sort of super spy," Vance said with a smirk. "We had a hard time reigning him in so he wouldn't attract too much attention."

"Was the plan for Gary to pass the galzium to Ellie?" Jill asked, hoping for more information.

"That was the original plan," Faye said. "I'm not sure what he planned by sending you to the disembarkation." Faye shook her head. "I saw you there too, but none of us knew enough to talk to each other."

"If you ask me, he was stupid," Vance said, turning to Faye. "It's time we go."

"Wait," Jill said. "Did you kill Gary and Danica?"

"No, we didn't," Faye said with a sigh. "Having the two of them die nearly unraveled our entire operation."

"We shouldn't volunteer anything else," Vance said as his eye darted to Faye. He stepped toward the door, and a moment later, they left.

The smugglers didn't kill Gary? she thought. *Should I even believe them? Did I miss something important?*

Jill detailed her meeting with Faye and Vance, speaking with Izzy and Kurt during afternoon tea.

"There was something about the way Faye talked," Jill said, placing her teacup on the coffee table. "I felt she was telling the truth when she said she didn't kill Gary or Danica."

"But they're smugglers," Izzy said with a look of concern on her face. "Their job is to lie so they can steal and get out of the messes caused by their thieving. You really can't trust anything she said."

"What you're saying makes sense," Jill said thoughtfully.

"Did you contact the IPS after they left?" Kurt asked.

Jill nodded.

Kurt eyed a small, round lemon tart topped with raspberries and blueberries. "Do you want another?"

Jill shook her head, although she enjoyed the tart. She could still taste the lemony sweetness from the one she'd eaten.

Kurt grabbed another and bit into it with a soft smile.

"I sent Harris a message as soon as the Overtons left," Jill said, swallowing the last of her tea. "He suspects they're not on Anteros any longer. Otherwise, why would they've visited me?"

"I'm afraid he's right," Izzy said, furrowing her brow.

"Why are you afraid of that?" Jill asked. "Doesn't that mean I'm safer?"

"Maybe," Izzy said. "Or it could mean someone else is in charge. The organization could still harm you if they think you have something they want."

"Didn't think—" Jill said before her comm chimed, interrupting her words. She activated it, causing a floating screen to appear. "It's a message from Leo. They're gathering everyone together; they've found something."

"That sounds interesting," Kurt said with a mouth full of lemon tart.

"Keep us in the loop," Izzy said, chuckling as she looked at Kurt.

Forty-five minutes later, Jill stepped through the Wilsons' double doors, into the entryway, and then the living room.

"Hey, Jill," Roman said, standing to meet her. "Are you okay after the memorial service?" He guided her to the nearest chair while he took a seat.

"Where is everyone?" Jill asked, glancing around the empty room.

"I'm here," Leo said, striding into the living room from another door. "I got... delayed." He plopped down on the couch and put his feet on the table. "Minnie's still in bed. She was upset after the service."

"That's why you asked..." Jill said, turning toward Roman.

"Yeah," Roman said, taking a sip from a fizzy pink drink. "Sorry, do you want one?"

Jill shook her head and suppressed a smile. He reminded her of Kurt, who was always eating.

"I was surprised she got so upset," Roman said.

"I wasn't," Leo said, pursing his lips. "She secretly dated Gary a few months ago. It didn't last long. He always had a new girlfriend waiting in line. Minnie didn't like that." He laughed, but there was no humor in it.

"Why didn't you tell me?" Roman asked, placing his half-empty glass on the coffee table with a clink.

Jill raised both eyebrows.

"I didn't want you to treat her differently," Leo said with a heavy sigh. "I still don't know if I should continue our relationship."

"But it's been... months?" Roman said. "And you're still thinking about it?"

Did Leo kill Gary? she thought.

Leo didn't respond but shifted uncomfortably in his chair.

"Is that why she's in bed?" Jill asked gently.

"Yeah," Leo said in a low voice. "I think she was in love with him."

"But you've dated for years," Roman said with indignation. "You can't continue like this."

"I know." Leo scowled. "I'm thinking about breaking up with her, but..."

The three of them sat in silence for a moment.

"We'll talk more later," Roman said, gazing steadily at his brother. He took a deep breath, exhaled slowly, and turned to Jill. "So, we invited you here for a reason; we heard from Faye and Vance."

Jill froze. *Were Izzy and Kurt right? Were these two now in charge of the smuggling ring?* she thought.

"Roman, I don't think this is a good idea," Leo said. "The less she knows, the safer we'll all be. Besides, she could go to the IPS."

"I want her to go to the IPS," Roman said. "The smuggling isn't going to stop. Whoever shows up next might decide we're in the way."

Leo pursed his lips but didn't reply.

"Occasionally," Roman began, "Leo and I helped Gary smuggle galzium out of the Spencer mines. At first, the only contact we had was Gary. Then he seemed to get more girlfriends than usual. It turned out Faye was actually his boss, but things seemed complicated with Danica. I think they were dating and smuggling the crystal."

"How long did you know Faye and Vance were behind the burglaries in our homes?" Jill asked.

"About a week after Gary died," Leo said, clearing his throat. "I'm sorry we couldn't tell you then."

"So, you, Roman, Angela, and Minnie casually discussed the break-ins," Jill said with an edge to her voice. "None of you thought to let me know."

"We were afraid of Faye and Vance," Roman said. "Leo and I assumed they'd killed Gary and later Danica."

"It wasn't exactly like that," Leo said. "Minnie and Angela didn't know about the smuggling...

well at least not in any detail. They would've been in trouble with Faye and Vance."

"Things changed again," Roman said, peering at Jill. "Faye visited us last night. She explained she was going to meet with you. She has left Anteros but didn't explain why. I had a feeling it was related to the couple of galzium shipments that were never delivered. She also encouraged us to tell you about the smuggling so that you'd inform the IPS."

Jill sighed, turning to Leo with narrowed eyes. "You know you'll be fired and may face jail time."

Leo nodded, and Roman rubbed the back of his neck.

"What if the IPS locks you two up?" Jill asked.

"We've already contacted our attorney," Leo said with a shrug. "They made an appointment with the IPS for two days from now. But Faye recommended going through you and then contacting an attorney."

"I suppose that'll ensure you get Harris," Jill said. "Also, I think contacting the IPS now instead of later would make you look better in their eyes."

"Let's contact Harris now," Jill said, looking from Leo to Roman. "The faster we do this, the safer we'll be." She pressed a button on her comm, starting a new vidchat.

CHAPTER 17

T he following afternoon, Jill bent over her creation, subtly adjusting the shade of blue in the distant storm. Her digital painting was nearly finished, and she grinned, satisfied with her work. Just as she debated which shade of teal-blue to add to a wave crashing on a distant island, her comm chimed.

Jill gritted her teeth and refused to look at the bracelet.

Every thirty seconds or so, a new round of chimes interrupted her thoughts. "You've got to be kidding me," she said, scowling. Turning to her comm, she activated it, reading the name but not looking at the screen.

"Minnie, I'm in the middle of something," Jill said, focusing on her creation and not bothering to keep the irritation out of her voice.

"I'm sorry," Minnie said in a quavery voice. "I just wondered if you'd heard about Spencer Industries."

Jill turned to the floating screen and took in Minnie's face, sad eyes, and watery smile.

"Uhmm...No," Jill said gently. "What happened?"

"The entire mining operation was shut down last night," Minnie said with a small smile. "I think things are finally coming to an end."

"What do you mean?" Jill asked, saving her composition and nudging its screen toward the wall.

"The IPS found the galzium vein," Minnie said. "It was in a newly excavated tunnel. The military is already working with the IPS to secure the vein. In the meantime, they're giving us a one-month vacation. I'm pretty sure after that, we'll all go back to work as usual. Oh, I'm sorry, I shouldn't have said that."

"I suppose that's good for everyone else," Jill said, as the corner of her mouth quirked up. "So, what's the real reason you've been trying to contact me?"

"Well..." Minnie said. "I thought we could get together and enjoy the time off work."

"Since I don't work for Spencer anymore, I'm not really on vacation," Jill said, leaning closer to the floating window, her eyes narrowing. "I'm not trying to be disrespectful, but what happened to the rest of your friends?"

Minnie's lower lip quivered, followed by quiet sobs as she tried to hide, stepping off-screen.

"I'm sorry. Forget I asked," Jill said, slightly panicked as something heavy settled in her chest.

Eventually, Minnie reappeared, wiping her eyes.

"I shouldn't have said that," Jill said in a quiet voice.

"No, it's okay," Minnie said, sniffling. "I deserve it. You see, since Leo and I grew up together, most of my friends are also his. A few months ago, I...you see, Gary and I..."

"It's okay," Jill said, holding up both hands. "Leo explained earlier."

"Oh, he told you, too," Minnie said with a sigh. "Well, Roman decided to tell all of our mutual friends, and they took Leo's side." She produced a watery smile. "So, right now, I don't have any friends. Also, it's okay if you have other plans today."

Jill gazed at the broken, watery-eyed woman for a moment. "How about I come over now?"

"Really?" Minnie said with a small smile. "I'd love that. But don't worry, I won't keep you for long."

Jill nodded as the floating screen went dark. She slowly exhaled, wondering what she'd gotten herself into.

About thirty minutes later, Jill took in the beautiful but sterile, manicured garden before reaching Minnie's house.

When Jill reached the top step, Minnie opened the door before the home's AI could greet her.

"Hey," Minnie said with a fresh face and a grin. She stepped forward, wrapped an arm around Jill's, and escorted her into the foyer, down the hallway, and into the living room.

"I have everything ready," Minnie said, gesturing to the tea and cakes. There were small, square pink sponge cakes in raspberry, cherry, and strawberry.

"That looks delicious," Jill said, taking a seat opposite Minnie. She popped one square in her mouth. "Mmm, strawberry's my favorite."

They talked more about Spencer and the galzium, but there really wasn't any new information. Instead, there was a lot of speculation.

"Spencer Industries' CEO, Henry Stone, has already made a public apology," Minnie said, placing her empty cup on the coffee table. "It looks pretty bad for them."

"Well, I'm happy to be away from it all," Jill said. "I'll continue working on my art and sell pieces when I can."

"I used to have friends who would've liked your art," Minnie said with a sad smile.

Jill didn't know how to reply and took the last swallow of tea before placing her cup on the coffee table.

"There's another reason I invited you here," Minnie said, shifting in her seat. "I don't have proof, but I'm pretty sure—"

"Leo Wilson is at the front door," the AI said, interrupting her.

"Leo," Minnie yelped, with a tiny squeal as she shot to her feet.

A wave of relief washed over Jill, who thought this was an excellent time to leave the two of them alone to talk. She stood, following Minnie.

Minnie, a broad grin on her face, raced to the front door, reaching it before Jill even exited the living room.

Suddenly, something heavy crumpled to the floor.

"Minnie?" Jill asked as she rounded the corner. She froze, taking in Minnie's lifeless body with a hole in the middle of her chest. The figure in front of her was clad from head to toe in a red-and-white Spencer Industries mining suit. It looked like the cloth uniform Jill had worn to work, but this one comprised a hard outer surface that covered every part of the wearer's body.

"Emergency," the home's AI announced. "The IPS has been contacted and will arrive in seven minutes."

It took several seconds for Jill to process what she was looking at. It was obviously not Leo; the mining suit figure was too short. But really, her first issue was the blaster pointed directly at her.

Jill yelped, spun on her heel, and raced back into the living room. Just then, a vase in the hallway next to where she'd been standing exploded. She spotted a door on the other side of the room and dashed toward it. Racing through the door, she nearly lost her balance as part of the wall exploded.

She found herself in a new hallway but couldn't figure out which way to go.

"Where is the back door?" Jill asked frantically, turning left and right.

"There is no back door," the AI responded in a cool, detached voice. "This house and the neighboring one share a wall."

Trying to figure out which way to go, she turned left and sped down the hall, where she found an enormous, modern bedroom. There were no doors, but she found three two-meter-high windows. Sprinting to the windows, she tried to pry them up, but they wouldn't budge.

"Please," Jill said, her voice tight. "Open the window."

"Only family members can issue commands that may compromise the home's safety."

"But this is an emergency!" Jill whisper-yelled. She froze hearing heavy footsteps plodding closer. Slowly spinning on her heel, she scanned the room for an idea. Gasping when her eyes fell on the ornate, metal lamp, she took large strides to a side table. She wrestled the brass-colored lamp into her arms and ran toward the nearest window, hurling it through the glass. The window disintegrated into tiny glass chunks. Jamming her entire leg through the window, she straddled the open window with one leg resting on the bedroom floor and the other on the lawn outside. Suddenly, the top windowpane disappeared with a bang, and she yelped as she fell through the window's remaining shards.

Whimpering at the deep cut in her leg, she did her best to ignore the pain as she forced herself to get up. Jogging and hopping through the side yard, she rounded the corner just as the bush next to her evaporated. Once in the front yard, she spotted two IPS hovercars drifting to the ground while she continued to limp toward them. She glanced behind her a few times, expecting to see the red-and-white attacker, but they never appeared.

Agent Swales was the first out of the hovercar, and although he was fuller around the middle, he moved surprisingly fast. Carrying her into the floating car, he set her down. The hovercar had a dark gray interior divided into two compartments. The front had room for a driver and passenger, while the back comprised two rows of seats for eight people. A passageway connected the two sections.

Jill sat on one seat in the back area with her bleeding leg outstretched. She trembled so much that it was difficult for Swales to scan her leg and then changed a setting on the scanner to knit her wound closed to stop the bleeding.

Through the hovercar's open door, Jill watched five agents enter Minnie's house with one stopping by her body. The remaining four disappeared into the house.

Now that the door was open, Jill's eyes fell on Minnie's body as hot tears began to trail down her face.

A couple of hours later, more IPS agents arrived to collect evidence, analyze the home's AI, and contact Minnie's relatives. Izzy and Kurt arrived separately. Izzy entered the hovercar, sitting next to Jill, while Kurt talked to some agents about the case.

Jill collapsed into Izzy's arms when she stepped into the hovercar.

"Would you like to step back into the house?" Agent Harris asked, standing at the entrance to the hovercar. "You might be more comfortable."

"No." Jill shook her head violently. The thought of going anywhere near the front door made her nauseous.

"Do you need to question her now?" Kurt asked, stepping toward the hovercar. "Can't you see she's upset?"

"You're only here as a courtesy," Agent Leigh said in a stern voice. She stood behind Kurt, arms crossed, and glared at him.

Kurt smirked and turned away.

Harris climbed into the hovercar, taking the seat across from Jill and Izzy. He brought up a floating screen and requested permission to record them.

"Would you tell me what happened here?" Harris asked.

Jill gripped Izzy's hand as she explained the reason for the visit, how someone had shown up at the door, but the AI had said it was Leo Wilson. The person who shot Minnie then chased her through the house. Jill paused, taking a deep breath trying to calm down.

"That sounds like the advanced tracking armor," Kurt said, frowning. "You can set it with a convincing false identity. It's extremely difficult to get one."

Izzy nodded.

"Why do you two know so much?" Harris asked, narrowing his eyes.

Izzy shifted uncomfortably in her seat while Kurt averted his eyes.

"Why do you think the killer came after you and Ms. Boothe?" Harris asked.

"I really don't know," Jill said with a sigh. "Minnie was going to tell me something, but the AI interrupted her. Maybe they came after me because they didn't want any witnesses..." She shrugged.

"Do you have any idea who the killer could be?" Harris asked, adding notes to his floating window.

"I think the killer has to be the person who mined the galzium to begin with," Kurt said, his mouth set in a straight line. "That would explain the Spencer mining suit she described."

"I'm talking to Ms. Solis," Harris said in a firm voice. "If you can't be quiet, please step away from the vehicle."

Kurt rolled his eyes and joined some agents standing a couple of meters away.

"He's just trying to protect Jill," Izzy said, shaking her head.

"Is there anything else you'd like to add?" Harris asked, ignoring Izzy.

"No," Jill said, still gripping Izzy's hand. "I just want to go home."

"Well, you should spend at least one night with us," Izzy said. "I don't think you should be alone tonight."

"I second that," Kurt said, joining them again. "Who knows, maybe someone here will give us a ride home."

Harris glared at Kurt for a moment before exiting the hovercar.

"You okay with staying with us for one night?" Izzy asked.

"Yeah," Jill said, trying to suppress a shiver. "I just want to leave."

A few minutes later, Agent Swales joined them.

"I have permission to take you home," he said.

Kurt grinned and jumped into the back of the hovercar as Swales climbed in and sat at the controls.

Jill took a deep breath as the hovercar drift-ed away from Minnie's home. The heaviness in Jill's chest returned as she thought about Min-nie—she didn't deserve to be murdered in her own home. She wondered how Leo, Roman, and Angela would take the news. *Why would some-one want to kill Minnie?*

CHAPTER 18

The following morning, Jill sat at the dining room table, cradling a warm cup of coffee. She stared down at the table while Izzy and Kurt's conversation washed over her.

"You're not allowed to wear that monstrosity in public," Izzy said in mock anger. "Where do you even find these things?"

"You just don't have any taste," Kurt said with a smirk. "This is the latest fashion from Tymal."

The corner of Jill's mouth twitched as she glanced again at Kurt's gaudy striped gold-and-red formal hat.

"Do you see what I have to put up with?" Izzy said with a lopsided smile.

Jill chuckled softly as the tension eased from her shoulders.

"Do you have plans today?" Kurt asked, taking a sip of tea.

"Not really," Jill said, slightly frowning. "I've been thinking about Gary, Danica, and Minnie. Why would someone kill them?"

"Something probably went wrong among the smugglers," Kurt said.

"Minnie wasn't involved with the smuggling," Jill said.

"That you know of," Izzy said. "Any one of them could've been lying to you."

"When Faye and Vance broke into my house," Jill continued, "they claimed they hadn't killed anyone."

"Well, we know they're liars," Izzy scoffed.

"That's the thing, though," Jill said. "Why kill someone who's making you rich? It didn't sound as if they had a falling-out."

"You mentioned Minnie seemed upset at the funeral," Izzy said. "But Gary's actual family seemed distracted and ready to leave."

"Yesterday..." Jill cleared her throat, trying to keep from crying. "Minnie seemed genuinely hurt by losing Leo and her friends." She gasped. "I just remembered Minnie was going to tell me something, but she didn't have proof."

"What do you think that was about?" Kurt asked.

"I think it was important," Jill said, tilting her head. "I think the real reason Danica and Minnie are dead has to do with Gary. Everything makes more sense when you look at the deaths as if they're related to Gary. Both Danica and Minnie were... intimate with him. Even though Leo and Roman mentioned Faye as a girlfriend, after meeting her, it just didn't feel that way."

"Oh, I'm beginning to understand," Kurt said. "But even though there's a connection, what would be the motive?"

"I was also thinking about who showed up at the funeral," Jill said. "Gary's family was there, but they seemed to be there out of obligation. The people most upset were Minnie, Angela, and maybe Leo. Since Minnie's gone, the remaining two might become the next victims."

"What about you?" Kurt asked.

"I only spent time with them to play Mystery Adventures," Jill said. "But the rest spent much more time together without me."

"So you're thinking of people close to Gary," Izzy said. "But the thing they all had in common was the smuggling."

"Not really," Jill said, shaking her head. "Leo, Roman, and Danica were involved in smuggling the galzium, but Angela, Minnie, and I weren't.

Also, Roman, maybe Leo, and I weren't upset at the funeral."

"Are you saying Leo or Roman might be the killers?" Kurt asked.

"Maybe," Jill said, blowing out a breath. "I still can't figure it out. What would be their motive?"

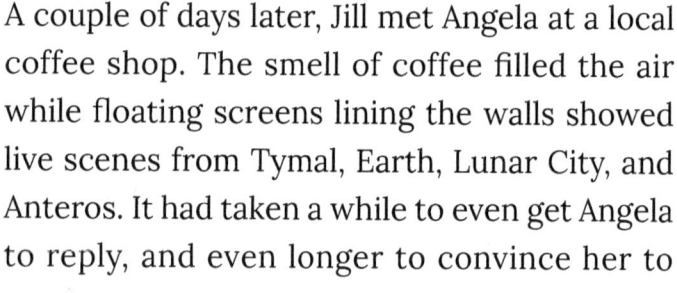

A couple of days later, Jill met Angela at a local coffee shop. The smell of coffee filled the air while floating screens lining the walls showed live scenes from Tymal, Earth, Lunar City, and Anteros. It had taken a while to even get Angela to reply, and even longer to convince her to meet.

"So you cornered me into this," Angela said, her mouth set in a grim line. "What do you want?"

Jill exhaled and studied Angela—she really looked at her. She noticed the dark circles under her eyes, the tension in her shoulders, and something else—maybe fear.

"I know we didn't end on the best terms," Jill said, quickly adding, "but I don't blame you for any of it. You were just doing your job."

She watched as Angela's shoulders relaxed and some of the tension left her face.

Angela swallowed some coffee.

"I really want to discuss Gary," Jill said.

Angela flinched, and Jill let the silence pass, hoping Angela would start talking about him.

"I know you, Leo, Roman, Minnie, and Danica formed a tight-knit group," Jill said. "It worries me that three of your group are dead now. I just wonder if one of you could be next."

"I don't understand why you're asking questions," Angela said, balling a fist. "Isn't that a job for the IPS?"

"Yes," Jill said, watching Angela's reactions. "But they're very focused on finding the smugglers. I think it's time we looked in new directions. Maybe the motive is actually credits like the IPS thinks. But it could be jealousy, love, anger, or greed."

Angela gazed at the screen showing Lunar City's Central Park, which depicted thick green foliage broken up by walkways and dotted with families.

"You're right that the IPS should be looking into this," Jill said, turning briefly to the same screen before continuing. "But a couple of days ago, I was also a target. I can't wait for the IPS to figure things out."

"What do you want from me?" Angela asked, blowing out a breath.

"Is there anyone else the group met with regularly?" Jill asked, taking a sip of coffee. This time, she waited longer for Angela's reply.

"We spent a lot of time with Faye, Vance, and once Ellie," Angela said, her eyes meeting Jill's. "Do you think they're in danger, too?"

"Ellie? Gary's sister?" Jill asked. "I didn't know you all hung out with her."

"Only once," Angela said. "She was part of the smuggling, maybe. But I didn't even know what they were up to until Gary…"

"There's something else I can't see bonding you all together," Jill said with a slight frown. "Which of them was part of the smuggling?"

"I'm not entirely sure," Angela said, examining her coffee. "I only heard things here and there from Leo, Roman, and Minnie, who were clearly involved. But I think Ellie, as I mentioned, along with Gary, Faye, and Danica."

"But Minnie didn't know about the smuggling," Jill said.

Angela shrugged a shoulder.

"What happened when you did spend time together?" Jill asked.

"It was always for a party," Angela said, with a wistful note in her voice.

"Did anyone else show up besides the ones we've discussed?" Jill asked.

"No," Angela said, tilting her head. "But I know they met at other times and didn't invite me."

"How do you know?" Jill asked.

"They'd mention other people and places I'd never visited," Angela said, waving a hand dismissively. "I didn't care; I was busy with work, anyway."

Something about the way Angela's eyes shifted led Jill to think it really bothered her. It also bothered Jill to know the entire department regularly spent time together and rarely included her.

"Look," Angela said after downing the last of her coffee. "Is there anything else? I need to get going."

"No, you've been helpful," Jill said. A moment later, she watched Angela take large strides out of the café and wondered what she was hiding.

Later that afternoon, Izzy, Kurt, and Jill walked around the neighborhood park. They strolled among shouts from happy children, sharp sounds from a racket hitting a ball, and old ladies sitting on benches tittering to each other.

Jill told them about her meeting with Angela.

"What was your impression of her?" Izzy asked, holding hands with Kurt.

"She seemed nervous," Jill said, tilting her head. "And fearful. Honestly, I had the distinct impression she was hiding something from me. But I didn't ask the right questions, or something."

"I wonder what she's not saying," Kurt said as he strutted with his gaudy gold-and-red striped hat. "When you mentioned her after your meeting, we started looking into her past. She's related to Gary, but they're fourth cousins. Like Gary, she came from a wealthy family, but it's not clear what happened after her father's death. Although they're related, she met Gary when she was twenty-six, and he was twenty-three. After meeting at a family function, they quickly became friends, and later, she hired him."

"I did some digging, too," Izzy said with a sly smile. "Did you know her dad used to buy and sell weapons for collectors? The entire collection was sold off around the time her dad passed, but what if she held on to a... blaster, for example?"

"I see what you mean," Jill said, her smile grim. "I wonder if her dad taught her how to use some of the weapons? Also, it's not easy to own a weapon in Anteros; she'd need a long list of government approvals and permissions."

"You realize about a third of Anteros citizens own weapons," Kurt said dryly. "They just own them illegally."

"But they tend to be connected with the gambling casinos," Jill said, "which leads us back to Gary."

They paused at a small pond and took in the foliage growing into the water.

"I thought Leo and Roman also gambled," Izzy said, reaching down to run her fingers through the water.

"Isn't that cold?" Jill asked, wrapping her arms around her torso.

"Freezing," Izzy said, standing and snuggling with Kurt.

"Roman doesn't gamble," Jill said. "Leo gambled a little with Gary before pulling away. I wonder if that was related to Minnie."

Jill turned away to continue their stroll around the park. She liked it when Izzy and Kurt were cozy with each other; it reminded her of her parents.

"Anyway, unless they gambled huge sums," Kurt said, "I don't think they'd need a firearm."

They followed the path around a strategically placed boulder that served as a visual boundary between one end of the neighborhood and the park.

"Of course, Faye and Vance were smugglers," Jill said. "I'm sure they would've needed protection. But they're gone now."

They walked silently past a copse of trees.

"I feel like a failure," Jill said, sighing heavily. "I should've been able to save Minnie."

"There's an entire IPS organization that's working on this full time," Kurt said. "They weren't able to protect her and haven't made any headway. I think you're doing just fine."

Izzy gave Jill a gentle squeeze.

"Besides, you're talking to us, and we're researching for you," Izzy said. "With all of our friends involved, we still can't figure this out."

"I guess," Jill said and paused. "I wish she was here. We weren't close or anything, but seeing how she died—she didn't deserve that."

CHAPTER 19

J ill sprinted over the red soil of the Martian landscape. Dressed in dark green shorts and a lavender blouse, her sandals slipped on the unstable dust as she rounded a four-meter-tall boulder. She peeked behind her, expecting the killer, but she'd evaded them for now.

When she spotted the double doors to the funeral home, she dashed inside, checking that the doors latched behind her. She stared through the doors' glass panes, hoping to catch a glimpse of the murderer now that she was safe.

"Oh, it's about time," Ellie called as she rushed toward Jill. "We've been waiting for you." She wrapped an arm around Jill's and guided her through another set of double doors. As they stepped inside, Jill's eyes widened at the new formal black dress, black heels, and matching gloves that covered her body.

Am I dreaming? she thought, slowly becoming aware she was in her bedroom and at the funeral home at the same time.

Ellie led her down the walkway in a room packed with Gary's relatives. They made their way to a giant silver urn with intricate carvings etched on the sides. When Jill reached Gary's remains, Ellie disappeared.

Examining the intricate details on the urn, she wondered if it was a puzzle safe and how to open it. Suddenly, quiet sniffling caught her attention. When she turned, she spotted Danica and Minnie, very much alive, gently wiping away their tears. Angela took the seat next to them, joining them with muted sobs.

They're the only ones crying, she thought, taking in the stoic relatives surrounding them.

Jill finally drifted fully awake and gazed up at the ceiling.

What was that about? she thought.

After turning the dream over in her mind for an hour, her stomach rumbled. She needed breakfast, but she also needed income. A few years ago, she had nearly supported herself by selling her digital pieces. Now she might do better with her larger following and portfolio.

Today, she'd work on marketing her new line of visual memoirs. It would reflect the journey she'd taken to develop her current piece. She didn't have a name for it yet, but she wanted something dramatic.

Still in her soft pink pajamas, she made her way to the living room, where she selected a cup of coffee and toast for breakfast from the meal crafter. Taking a bite of the bread, she created a floating screen and looked at her digital paintings on commission in the Modern Muses Gallery. Her contract would end soon, and her digital art would most likely be removed.

She had set a showing date at The Red Frame Gallery. Contacting her patrons, she planned to send an invitation and provide more information about the visual memoirs.

Glancing through her list, she focused on her patrons in Anteros and even Lunar City. Then she began to carefully construct an invitation to a private viewing of her current composition. Two hours passed while she wrote and rewrote the invitation. Her remaining coffee turned cold while the toast was long gone. She reread it for the hundredth time as a broad smile slowly crept across her face.

Excellent! Maybe I don't need to keep working as an engineer, she thought.

She reviewed her list of patrons one last time and sent the message. Almost at the same time, her comm chimed. It was a notification from the Modern Muses Gallery, reminding her to collect her remaining credits. Since they'd moved her remaining paintings to the back walkway, where few people would see them, there was no reason to wait. Activating a floating screen, she entered her account at the gallery. She began acknowledging each of the few sales she'd received over the past month when she froze.

"Angela Newton?" Jill gasped. "What are you doing here?" A sinking feeling formed in the pit of her stomach.

Selecting Angela's name, she found she'd purchased a small piece called *Sunshine of the Soul*. It was one of Jill's earliest works, which she'd spent months creating. She'd taken her time painting just the right colors for every tiny flower, blade of grass, and insect that filled the bright, sunny meadow.

Angela had purchased that digital art piece the day Gary and Danica had died. She bought it from the Modern Muses Gallery on the second floor of the Ruby Sunset Hotel.

Jill's fingers trembled as she activated her comm.

"Good morning," Izzy's smiling face filled the screen.

Jill stared, trying to arrange her thoughts.

"What's wrong?" Izzy asked as her face fell.

"I just discovered where Angela was when Gary and Danica died," Jill said, doing her best to keep her voice steady. She explained that Angela had bought her composition from Modern Muses.

"That's on the second floor," Izzy said in a quiet but steady voice. "You have to pass the casino to get there."

"Or to leave," Jill added. "I'm sure it's designed that way to encourage more gambling."

"What do you think happened?" Kurt asked, joining their conversation.

"Angela purchased the picture, took those wide stairs down one flight, and ran into Gary and Danica gambling. If they were there because of the smuggling, they wouldn't have been able to tell her exactly why they were at the casino. Also, I'm pretty sure Gary and

Danica were... together, and they wouldn't have wanted her to know about that."

"But why not?" Kurt asked, furrowing his brows.

"I think Angela was in love with Gary," Jill said. "I have a feeling she didn't mind his previous girlfriends because they came and went. But Danica stuck around for a while."

"I suppose she killed Minnie, too," Izzy said. "Was it because she was in love with Gary?"

"Maybe..." Jill's voice trailed off. "The thing is, he was already dead—there was no motive. Also, if she was the killer at the door, it was rushed, even a little sloppy."

"So was the murder at the Ruby Sunset," Kurt said, scratching his chin. "It doesn't seem as if anything was thought out."

"Right now, I think we should contact the IPS," Izzy said. "Do you want to contact Harris, or should we do it together like last time?"

"Let's do it together," Jill said. "I'll shower and meet you at your apartment."

Izzy and Kurt nodded before their screen went dark.

Jill took a deep breath and closed the floating window, lost in thought. After a moment, she cleared her coffee table and got ready to leave her house.

Thirty minutes later, Jill adjusted her dark purple shirt and black pants before turning to the front door. It slid open, and Jill gasped as she stared at a red-and-white Spencer mining suit holding a blaster. The figure stepped closer, placing a thin tube over Jill's ear. She reached for it, and the red-and-white suit pointed the blaster at her forehead.

The figure stepped even closer to Jill, causing her to scramble backward. The red-and-white suit entered her house, and the door slid shut. Jill's mind refused to work as she fixated on the weapon.

The two of them stood still, facing each other when Jill's mind slowly began to thaw out.

"Angela?" Jill asked. "Are you going to kill me, too?"

The mining suit shifted the blaster to its left hand, and the right one removed the helmet.

Angela's blonde hair framed her face as it fell to her shoulders. Her lips were set in a grim line as she glared at Jill.

"I wondered how long it would take you to notice my purchase," Angela said. "The gallery alerted me as soon as you moved my credits to your account."

"What?" Jill stammered.

"Shut up!" Angela yelled. "I only bought that stupid painting to help you out. I didn't realize my mistake for a few days, but the IPS missed it completely. Sit down!"

Jill scrambled backward to her sofa and sat on the edge with a straight back and stiff shoulders.

"I knew firing you was a bad idea," Angela said, scowling. "It'd give you too much time to meddle. But I couldn't talk my boss out of it." She blew out a sharp breath.

Angela grabbed the seat opposite Jill and continued pointing the blaster at her.

"I have to kill you," Angela said, pursing her lips. "But I haven't figured out where to do it yet."

"You don't have to, you know," Jill said, desperately trying to think of something to stay alive. "With the tracking armor you put over my ear, nobody knows I'm here. I could wait a day, or however long you need, to give you time to leave Anteros."

Angela chuckled.

That laugh sent shivers down Jill's spine. She'd seen Angela's steely side at work—reprimanding coworkers, arguing schedule adjustments with the miners, and even occasionally correcting her boss. That chuckle was just one of many clues that she wouldn't change her mind.

"How did you kill Gary and Danica?" Jill asked, squeezing her hands together to hide their trembling. "Casinos have cams everywhere."

"I never entered the casino," Angela said with a bitter laugh. "They met in front of the gallery, Gary coming from the casino and Danica from the hotel. I saw them kissing and knew... Anyway, I followed her back to her apartment. She confessed to seeing Gary for months, and I... got rid of her."

"Since Danica was dead, why kill Gary?" Jill asked, clearing her throat and trying to buy time. Izzy and Kurt would eventually realize something was wrong.

"I could take you outside the city dome," Angela said, narrowing her eyes. "If I pushed you out of my hovercar, you'd die instantly of exposure."

"You have a hovercar?" Jill asked, genuinely surprised. "They're so expensive."

"Yes, well..." Angela said in a distracted voice. "My father left it to me."

"I understand your dad was a weapons dealer," Jill said, trying to engage her in another way.

"Shooting you now is out of the question," Angela said, pursing her lips. "I made that mistake with Minnie. But it'd be too difficult to disguise and transport your body. I don't have the right tools."

Jill racked her brain, trying to think of something new to draw Angela's attention.

"I could poison you," Angela said, smirking as she glanced around the room. "You probably have enough cleaning chemicals to pull it off. If you die differently, the IPS might think your murder isn't related."

"Did you love Gary?" Jill asked gently, coming up with another way to distract her. "He lied, and I suppose, he never loved you."

Angela's head snapped toward Jill, and her eyes watered. "Shut up!"

Jill flinched, but Angela shot to her feet and paced around the sofa, glaring at her.

"Who told you about us?" Angela asked, her voice edged with tension.

"Nobody," Jill said in a soft voice she would've used to console a friend. "The only people upset about Gary's death were you and Minnie. Leo told me Minnie was in love with Gary. That made me wonder about you."

Angela paced in silence for a while, intermittently glaring at Jill and staring at the ground.

Jill thought about using her comm to contact Izzy, but she'd need to remove the tracking armor and Angela would notice it.

"My dad was a paid killer for some of the local casinos," Angela said. "I know you've been talking to Leo, Roman, and even the IPS. None of them knows about my dad. He taught me enough to defend myself, but refused to fully train me. Instead, he wanted me to have a normal life, whatever that means. But he left me a few weapons and a code. I can kill if someone hurts me, but I can't kill innocents."

"You mean I'm alive because I haven't hurt you?" Jill asked, wide-eyed.

Angela stopped pacing, the blaster still pointed at her.

"I had a tough decision," Angela said, closely eyeing her. "If I let you go to the IPS, you'd be harming me, and I could kill you. But then the IPS would come for me. I thought I could force myself to kill you."

"Well, I guess I'm glad for your dad's ethics," Jill said with a forced laugh.

"I still have to kill you," Angela said and smirked.

"Didn't Gary mention the smuggling?" Jill asked, squeezing her hands tighter and hoping to delay Angela as much as possible. "I'm only asking because you were in a relationship."

"Gary was a liar," Angela said matter-of-factly. "He lied to get himself out of trouble and to cause problems for others. He also lied when he didn't need to." She sighed and seemed to deflate a little. "He knew I didn't casually break rules, and if he'd told me about the smuggling, I would've tipped off the IPS myself. He and Danica were in it together, but neither of them was smart enough to organize something that complex. When I asked who else was involved, they refused to talk."

"Minnie didn't really hurt you," Jill said. "Why kill her?"

"She was nosy," Angela said, gritting her teeth. "Minnie fell in love with Gary, but he suddenly dumped her. Then she stalked him for a few weeks before discovering me and Danica. Although Danica and I didn't know about each other, at least not until the night I killed her."

"I still don't see how she hurt you," Jill said.

"After Gary died, she guessed or figured out I was involved," Angela said, pursing her lips. "Then she tried to convince me to go to the IPS. I refused. But when she threatened to tell the IPS herself, she had to go." A steely glint shone in Angela's eyes.

Jill suppressed a shudder.

"Stand up," Angela said, waving the blaster toward the door. "I know where we're going now."

Jill ran through several ideas to keep the conversation going.

"I know you've been stalling," Angela said, scowling. "But nobody's coming. Now, get up!"

"Where are—" Jill said, climbing to her feet.

"You'll see soon enough," Angela said with a sneer.

Angela shoved her in the back, forcing her toward the door.

Jill stumbled but didn't lose her balance. Instead, she squared her shoulders and walked in steady, even strides.

CHAPTER 20

J ill led the way out of her house, following a footpath through the neighborhood. Angela jammed the blaster against her back as she walked in lockstep just behind.

"Don't even think of trying anything," Angela muttered under her breath.

Their footsteps echoed off the path past the neighboring houses.

"It's the middle of the morning," Jill said, forcing her voice into a steady cadence while scanning for passersby. "There are still people walking through the neighborhood or spending time at the park. Aren't you worried someone will see you or that thing you have pointed at my back?"

"Nope," Angela said with a chuckle. "First, nobody ever notices anything. As long as you don't do something to attract attention, nobody will even remember seeing you." She leaned forward and whispered in Jill's ear. "Don't get any ideas. I'm not afraid to drop you right now."

Despite forcing a calm voice and steady steps, Jill's fingers trembled. But with Angela's threat that moment of fear transformed into clenched fists.

"Second," Angela said in a light, conversational tone, "only the AIs controlled by the IPS pose any real threat. Both of us are wearing tracking armor, and even my blaster's shielded."

A few minutes later, they emerged from the neighborhood and came to a small two-seater hovercar sitting partially on the residential walkway and partway on a larger path that surrounded the nearby park.

"What?" Jill said with wide eyes. "How did you get an IPS transport?"

Angela chuckled. "It's only marked as an IPS transport, but people are likely to ignore it."

A mom and two little boys emerged from a nearby walkway. The boys raced across the path surrounding the park while the mom jogged behind them. Glancing at the IPS markings on the vehicle, the mom followed her children, who only had eyes for the playground.

As Jill and Angela approached, the driver and passenger doors slid into pockets in the hover-car's walls.

"Get in," Angela said, her face morphing into a stony expression. "I'm still not afraid to kill you right now."

They walked to the passenger side, and Jill climbed in. The door engaged and locked. Angela hid the blaster and headed for the driver's door.

"Glad you didn't try anything," Angela said with a smirk. "It would've been messy to kill you now, but I'd still do it."

It wasn't that Jill hadn't considered escaping. She'd thought about activating the vehicle's controls, locking Angela out, and contacting the IPS. But she stared at the control panel with wide eyes.

"How do you fly this thing?" Jill said, her brows furrowed. "There aren't any manual controls."

"This is a prototype," Angela said, settling into her seat as the driver's door closed and they floated higher into the city's dome. "This is one of only seven. It works with Askovian brain-waves. But this particular model is designed for Readers."

"I can't believe this isn't widely used," Jill said, scanning the dashboard again.

"How do you know it's not widely available?" Angela asked, raising one eyebrow. "The military owns the patent, and the inventor had permission for only seven personal vehicles."

"The military, of course," Jill said quietly, watching the direction of their flight. "I suppose we're leaving the city."

"Not quite," Angela said, tapping her comm to bring up a private floating screen.

Jill couldn't see the contents of her screen, but wondered if some aspects of flying the car couldn't be done with Reader abilities.

They approached a part of Anteros that Jill had only visited with her parents when she was a child. It was the farmers' depot where growers and buyers exchanged crops for credits. Her parents had wanted her to understand where the food came from that fed everyone.

The hovercar descended into an open space in the middle of a complex maze of warehouses and long chains of floating trains. Jill remembered her awe as the tour guide had explained that some trains headed to other colonies on Mars, while most headed off-world to mines on other moons. The trips varied from a few days to Mar's moon, Phobos, to a couple of months to Jupiter's moon, Ganymede.

Suddenly, the image of Danica lying beside an empty container, flashed into Jill's mind. She sat on her hands to stop them from trembling. Her mind turned sluggish as the realization settled in. *This might be her last hovercar ride.*

"I told you my dad refused to teach me to be an assassin," Angela said with a wistful smile. "But I still learned the trade. I followed his friends, who thought I was too young to understand. When I had questions, I asked his old buddies, who assumed my dad was training me in the family business. Of course, I only got away with that for a few years before Dad caught on and sent me to Earth to learn to be a competent Reader."

"You know you still don't have to do this," Jill said, trying to keep the panic out of her voice.

"I think I've found the perfect place for you," Angela said with a malicious grin. "I located a partially filled container heading for Lunar City."

Jill turned toward the side window. *I have to escape*, she thought.

A moment later, the hovercar touched the ground, and a thin cloud of red dust floated into the air.

"Now, let me see," Angela said, peering at the floating screen again. "We need to go to sections L-eleven and twelve."

"The depot will have tons of farmers and buyers," Jill said, her voice pinched. "We'll be seen."

"Most people won't pay attention to two random people crossing the depot," Angela said as both doors slid open. "You're still wearing tracking armor, so security can't monitor you. Don't even think about removing it."

Jill climbed out while Angela shot out of her seat and jogged to the open passenger door.

A thin layer of red dust covered most buildings. This part of Anteros wasn't paved over like the rest of the city. Several trains floated into a nearby, grungy, dust-covered warehouse. Security guards strolled by with their heads buried in floating screens. In the distance, three or four engineers in green uniforms ambled out of a three-story office building with purposeful strides.

"Where's the blaster?" Jill asked, gazing at Angela's hands.

"Shut up and walk," Angela said curtly.

"So," Jill replied, "even though regular citizens aren't very aware of their surroundings, trained engineers and security guards are. Is that why you can't show your weapon?"

"Keep walking," Angela said with an edge in her voice.

Following Angela's instructions, Jill strolled into a dusty alleyway between the grungy warehouse and a newer-looking, enormous building.

"Faster," Angela whispered harshly. "I don't have all day."

Jill picked up her pace until she was just below a full run. Hearing Angela huffing and puffing behind her, she grinned.

A moment later, Jill emerged from the alley and sprinted toward the floating train she'd seen entering the adjacent warehouse. It moved at a slow pace, similar to a stroll in the park. Remembering she'd seen the end of this train approaching as they'd landed, Jill's legs pumped harder. She rounded the end of the train and turned to enter the warehouse.

The lighting inside was dimmer than she expected, and a moment later, she realized why. A long row of robotic arms reached into the slow-moving train, selecting large, cube-shaped containers and placing them on a conveyor belt heading deeper into the ware-house.

Robots don't need light, she thought. These arms reminded her of the mining arms at her job, except these were four times larger. One thing she knew about these mechanical appendages: they always had lots of open spaces to allow for easier maintenance, which now meant she had places to hide. She continued dashing along the outside of the row of robotic arms.

"Jill!" Angela yelled. "Get back here!"

Diving between two robots, Jill scooted into the narrow space between the mechanical arms and the slow-moving, floating train. She ran intermittently in spurts, coming to sudden stops so that the robot arms and train wouldn't crush her.

"Jill!" Angela shouted.

Gasping, Jill shuffled her feet faster, and now she had a new problem. The end of the train was approaching, and that would allow Angela to find her. She turned to the train before making her decision.

Bending her knees, she pushed off, leaping toward the train. She grasped a hold bar and scrambled between the last two train cars. Squeezing onto a narrow platform, she made her way to the opposite side of the car, hoping Angela wouldn't think to check there. She shuffled as quickly as possible along the second-to-last car until she reached the one ahead. Continuing forward for several more cars, she stopped when the train exited the warehouse.

"Jill!" Angela's voice echoed in the warehouse. "Jill!"

Sighing with relief, she allowed herself to relax just a little. Jill removed her tracking armor while focusing on the buildings as the train passed. When it approached the large, three-story office building, she jumped off, stumbled, and fell to her knees. But it wasn't over yet.

She raced toward the central building and sprinted inside, nearly colliding with two engineers leaving the building, but she couldn't stop. When Angela left the warehouse, Jill would be in danger again. A moment later, she reached a large, semicircular desk where a heavyset woman leaned back in her chair, propping her feet on the desk, and watching an entertainment serial on a floating screen.

"Please alert the IPS," Jill said, out of breath. "Someone's trying to kill me."

"Jill? It's so good to see you again," Faye said, stepping closer with a stiff smile.

"Yes, we weren't expecting you," Vance said, approaching from the opposite direction.

Jill's stomach dropped.

The heavyset woman pulled her feet off the desk. "You two know what this is about?" she asked, looking from Faye to Vance.

Jill opened her mouth to reply, but Faye shook her head with a slight motion.

"Yes, we'll take care of this," Vance said with a broad smile.

Doris nodded, turning back to her serial.

Faye and Vance frog-marched Jill further into the building while her heart hammered in her chest. They made their way down a dingy hall that looked as if it hadn't been dusted in a while. Although, given how dusty it was outside, the other engineers probably brought it in on their boots.

Once inside, they forced Jill into a chair and took the seats on either side.

"I just want to be completely clear," Faye said in a matter-of-fact tone. "We won't harm you."

Jill's eyes locked with Faye's. She didn't receive a mental message from Faye, but for some reason, Jill believed her.

"We've been tracking you," Vance said, glancing at Faye. "We thought the real killer would eventually come after you, Angela, Leo, or Roman."

"Imagine our surprise when we discovered *Angela* was the murderer," Faye said with a grim smile.

"What... what are you doing here?" Jill asked, trying hard to make sense of her day so far.

"You've handed the IPS our last two galzium shipments," Faye said casually, as if discussing the weather. "Our first package was that puzzle box you turned over to the IPS. Gary planned to turn it over to us the day he died. The second was that collection of galzium crystals you found at work. If Gary had been alive, he would've collected them."

"What do you want from me?" Jill asked, fighting to keep her voice steady.

"We need the killer," Faye said with a smile that didn't reach her eyes. "Our organization doesn't allow mistakes unless you take steps to fix them."

"Well, she's out there in a warehouse," Jill said in a raised voice. "If you hurry, you might still catch her."

"Calm down," Faye said, patting her hand, looking Jill up and down. "We'll bring her to our bosses. You see, not only did she cause the loss of two galzium parcels, she killed two valuable operatives."

Jill pulled her hands away from Faye's and leaned farther into her chair.

"Now tell me," Faye said, "are you injured? How did you get away from that blaster?"

Jill took a deep breath and launched into her tale of how Angela had found her at home, forced her into the hovercar, and brought her to the farmers' depot. She even explained a little of Angela's past.

Faye and her husband looked at each other and laughed.

"I think the problem is we've been underestimating you and Angela from the very beginning," Faye said.

"Is that why you treated my home differently from the others?" Jill asked.

"Ironically, we spent the least amount of time with you and Angela," Vance said. "Instead, we focused on the rest of Gary's friends and even his relatives. They were... uncomplicated."

"So, did Ellie take part in the smuggling?" Jill asked.

"We can't answer that," Faye said with a sneer.

"I see," Jill said hesitantly. "The IPS is looking for you, but you met me in the open lobby. Anyone could've seen you."

"Let's just say we have connections," Vance said with a smirk.

"Let go of me!" Angela yelled from outside the conference room. "You can't hold me! You're not the IPS!"

Suddenly, the door slid open, and two large men in engineering uniforms held both of Angela's arms as they forced her into the room.

"I'm not talking to any of you!" Angela shouted.

Faye stood, narrowing her eyes at Angela, whose shouts slowed and then stopped. Her eyes drooped, and her whole body went limp. The guards carried her to the nearest chair.

"Well, Jill," Faye said, turning to face her. "This is where we part ways. Go back to the front desk and ask Doris to contact the Colburns. Please don't vidchat the IPS from here, or you'll involve our bosses. That won't go well for any of us." She set her face into a stony expression.

Jill climbed to her feet, taking a shaky breath. She paced toward the door, which slid open, and turned back to Faye.

"I don't suppose you can tell me what'll happen to her?" Jill asked.

"You really don't want to know, little one," a voice in Jill's head said. She nodded, turned, and stepped through the open door.

CHAPTER 21

Later that evening, Jill had taken a hot shower, eaten a delicious meal, and now cradled a warm cup of tea as she sat cross-legged on Izzy and Kurt's couch.

"Our contacts at the IPS confirmed Angela's disappearance," Kurt said, sitting across from Jill with a grim smile. "They only found her hovercar at the farmers' depot, and she's not at her house."

"I don't think anyone's going to find her," Izzy said, turning to Jill. "But how are you, really?"

"Okay, I guess," Jill said, shrugging a shoulder. "I can't get that scene out of my head. The way Faye and Vance looked at Angela. The way she glared back, knowing she was going to die..."

"But she was a murderer," Kurt said.

"I know," Jill sighed. "I think what's bugging me is, everybody in that room broke the law. It should've been the IPS that handled everyone." She let out a slow breath. "I feel like a bit of a coward for not alerting the IPS when I reached Doris's desk."

"I'm so grateful you didn't do that," Izzy said, placing her cup on a nearby table. "Otherwise, we'd be wondering what happened to you."

"Here on Anteros, some people are above the law," Kurt said, munching on a small, round cherry tart. "Do you remember that story of the Cartwrights?"

"She killed two Pendletons." Jill nodded. "Everyone knows, including the IPS, and yet she walks around freely."

"They must have some underworld ties," Izzy said. "I think it's safer to let this one go. Justice was served, in a way."

They sat quietly for a moment.

"Have you had a chance to talk to Roman and Leo?" Izzy asked.

"No," Jill said. "They left messages asking if I'd heard from Angela. But I haven't responded."

"What would you even say?" Izzy asked.

"I don't know," Jill said. "They worked with Faye and Vance; you'd think they'd already know about Angela."

"It could be a trap to see what you know," Kurt said, furrowing his eyebrows.

"I thought of that," Jill said. "I wasn't going to reply. Faye and Vance were more afraid of their bosses than the IPS. If the Wilsons try to contact me again, I won't admit to anything."

"On another note," Kurt said, "I just heard a branch of one of Spencer's mining locations is now permanently under military control. It's not too much of an impact financially, but they look weak now."

"I wonder what they'll do to cover up the military control?" Jill asked.

"Launch a PR campaign designed to make them seem like the saviors of humanity," Izzy said, chuckling.

"That's what Pendleton Mining did when the IPS caught them a few years ago," Kurt said, joining in the laughter.

After a lull in the conversation, Jill said, "I want to visit Earth. Not now, but in a couple of years. I've been recreating its landscapes from digital photos for years. Now I want to see it for myself."

"That's a great idea," Izzy said. "How long will you be gone?"

"I don't know," Jill said, tilting her head. "Maybe three to four years; it takes sixteen months just to travel there and back."

"My dear, we'll miss you," Izzy said with a gentle smile.

"Too bad we can't join you," Kurt said, swallowing the last of his tart. "But we have—"

"Something else planned," Izzy said, glancing at her husband.

"Yes," Kurt said. "Other plans."

"You have plans in a couple of years?" Jill asked, looking from Kurt to Izzy. "What's going on?"

"Uhmm..." Izzy said, shifting uncomfortably in her seat. "We can't discuss it, at least not yet."

Jill studied them, knowing they wouldn't give her any more explanation.

"When you visit Earth, start in Tymal," Kurt said. "I have a friend who could keep you safe. I'll let him know you're coming."

"More importantly, have fun," Izzy said with a grin. "Visit oceans, forests, deserts, and all the landscapes you can think of."

"There's no place more beautiful than Earth," Jill said. "I can't wait to create digital art while I'm surrounded by nature."

A month later, Jill strolled through the Red Frame Gallery. A bubbly excitement raced through her as she stopped by Veronica, the gallery owner.

"This showing is a huge success," Veronica said, leaning toward Jill's ear. They stood in the middle of the crowded floor. "I need to handle something in the office. I'll be back."

Jill nodded and turned to welcome a few patrons. After greeting and chatting for a few minutes, two new faces caught her attention.

"Leo, Roman," Jill said, a broad smile spreading across her face. "I'm so happy you could come."

"Wouldn't miss it," Roman said, chewing on a small chocolate hors d'oeuvre.

"We didn't realize you were so talented," Leo said in a quiet voice. "Minnie tried to get us to take a look at your art, but..."

A moment of silence settled among them.

"I miss her, too," Jill said, giving his hand a squeeze.

"But we're here to celebrate," Roman said, taking a sip of champagne. "Can you give us the grand tour?"

"Of course, follow me," Jill said, turning to a display of eight digital art pieces dominating the center floor. The first one they encountered was her latest piece. "I call it 'The Solitude in the Tempest.'" It was a bold composition showing a stormy sea with waves crashing on a beach framed by high, moody cliffs. In the distance, a lone island stood desolate in the roiling ocean.

"Wow," Leo said, his eyes widening. "I had no idea you were this good."

"Have you lived on Earth?" Roman asked, as his eyes slowly roamed over the digital canvas.

"No," Jill said with the confidence she'd learned from Kurt and Izzy. "I spent my childhood listening to stories from people who grew up on Earth. Their words created such vivid pictures in my mind. I knew I had to capture them in paintings."

"But, this is so accurate," a short, plump gray-haired woman added. "I lived in Tymal from childhood through my thirties, and you've captured the... feeling of the storm."

"Thank you," Jill said, slightly blushing. "When I first started painting, I would ask my parents or one of their friends if I'd captured the forests, mountains, or beaches they'd left behind. They offered feedback and showed me digital photos."

"Oh, that's it," Roman said, interrupting her explanation. "This is a copy of a digital photo."

"No, not at all," Jill said, chuckling. "Take a look at the neighboring display."

A small crowd had gathered while Jill spoke, and now all heads turned to the next display.

"This is a visual memoir of 'The Solitude in the Tempest,'" Jill said, her lips spreading a little wider. She stood a little straighter and raised her voice. "I started with an image of farmland at the base of Tymal. What you're looking at is a field of wheat."

More 'oohs' and 'ahhs' escaped the mouths of the delighted crowd.

"I started with the feeling from this image," Jill said with a confident smile. "I paid particular attention to the wave patterns in the wheat. Then I began my composition."

"Wow, the two look nothing alike," Leo said, tilting his head.

Roman nodded, and several other patrons murmured among themselves for several minutes.

"Would you like me to explain my next digital art piece?" Jill asked, beaming at the crowd. She continued the mini-tour of her artwork, thoroughly enjoying talking to her longtime supporters and the new ones who'd recently joined. *I had no idea this could be so much fun,* she thought.

***

To enjoy more cozy mystery science fiction, pick up Temple Shadows (https://katherines books.com/temple/).

PLEASE LEAVE AN HONEST REVIEW

A uthors thrive on reviews. These reviews help other readers decide whether to buy the book. To write a review, simply go back to the website where you purchased this book, provide a star rating, and add a couple of sentences explaining why you liked the book. Thank you for your review.

Amazon Review Link
(https://katherinesbooks.com/psmrevamz)

Would you like another Sci-Fi Whodunit?

Get early access to my upcoming books in the series when you join my newsletter. I also post more detail about characters, worlds, or interesting science fiction ideas. Don't miss out! Join now at:

https://katherinesbooks.com/scifi-short-story

Books

Standalone Books

The Puzzle Safe Mystery
https://katherinesbooks.com/psmamz
The Runaway Martian
https://katherinesbooks.com/runawaymartia
namz

***

The Feeler Series Books

The Feeler (Book 1)
katherinesbooks.com/feeler
Movers, Mines, and Murder (Book 2)
katherinesbooks.com/movers
Lunar Justice (Book 3)
katherinesbooks.com/lunarjustice
Spencer Legacy (Book 4)

katherinesbooks.com/spencerlegacy

ABOUT THE
AUTHOR

K atherine is a science fiction author who spent nearly thirty years working as an engineer before retiring and turning to her life-long love of storytelling. She grew up devouring classic sci-fi, especially the works of Isaac Asimov, Arthur C. Clarke, and Ray Bradbury. As much as she adored those stories, she often felt something was missing.

Over time, her reading tastes broadened to include cozy mysteries, thrillers, and fantasy. Eventually she realized her ideal book would be a blend of the genres she loved most. The solution was obvious: write cross-genre stories that fuse the wonder of science fiction with the charm and puzzle-solving of cozy mystery.

Katherine lives in New England, where she spends her days writing, reading, and enjoying time with her family.